BEARLY
IN
CONTROL

ALSO BY MILLY TAIDEN

Sassy Mates Series

Scent of a Mate
A Mate's Bite
Unexpectedly Mated
A Sassy Wedding
The Mate Challenge
Sassy in Diapers
Fighting for Her Mate

Federal Paranormal Unit

Wolf Protector
Dangerous Protector
Unwanted Protector

Black Meadow Pack

Sharp Change
Caged Heat

Paranormal Dating Agency

Twice the Growl
Geek Bearing Gifts
The Purrfect Match
Curves 'Em Right

Wynter's Captive

Sinfully Naughty Vol. 1

Club Duo Boxed Set

Don't Drink and Hex

Hex Gone Wild

Hex and Kisses

Alpha Owned

Bitten by Night

Seduced by Days

Mated by Night

Taken by Night

Match Made in Hell

BEARLY
IN
CONTROL

Shifter Undercover, Book One

MILLY
TAIDEN

Montlake
Romance

Published by Montlake Romance, Seattle

www.apub.com

Amazon, the Amazon logo, and Montlake Romance are trademarks of Amazon.com, Inc., or its affiliates.

ISBN-13: 9781503941564
ISBN-10: 1503941566

Cover design by Eileen Carey

Printed in the United States of America

For my girls: Tina and Julie. Your unwavering support is priceless.

CHAPTER ONE

Charli Avers sat in her SUV and shook her head at the scene before her: two morons behind the barn trying to drag something big and furry out of the back end of a horse trailer. She couldn't believe she got out of bed this early. Some emergency. She was kicking Fred's ass for this. Thank god it was Thursday. One more day.

Charli watched with disbelief as Fred backed a tractor to the trailer's open gate. What the hell were they doing now? Jed wrapped a rope around the tractor's hitch, then tied the line to the animal's leg sticking out. This would not end well.

The tractor's engine gave a low, grinding whine and the machine inched forward, pulling out the biggest black bear she had ever seen. Her jaw dropped. It was magnificent and scary as hell. For the two men's sakes, she hoped Fred was right about it being dead. If it wasn't, it could wake up and eat them in two bites.

Fred looked up from the tractor and waved her over. Charli reached into the backseat and grabbed her small veterinarian's bag, then heard screams outside the truck. She whipped her head around to see Jed circling the tractor with a black mass of fur and white teeth chasing him.

"Shoot it, Fred! Shoot it!" Fred stood on top of the farm equipment, laughing his ass off watching Jed run around. Charli groaned and got out of her truck. This was going to be a long day.

Fred had jumped down and claimed his rifle when she came around the barn's corner. She about choked. "Fred, put your gun down! Don't shoot."

"I's got to, Doc. It'll eat Jed, and I ain't doin' his chores for the rest of my life, dagnabit." He fired a shot that ricocheted off the trailer's fender and slammed into the chicken coop. Feathers and a parade of cackles erupted from the pen.

"Fred, stop. You'll kill someone!" *And never hit the bear.*

Jed, wide-eyed and screaming like a little girl, headed toward them in a dead run. The bear was close enough to swat at him. Fred lifted the rifle.

"I said no." Charli rushed the shooter, determined to have no deaths today, animal or human. She knocked the gun off target as it fired, but it wasn't enough and the bullet sank into black fur. The bear stopped and turned murderous eyes toward them. He roared, jaw flashing wide. Charli turned fully to the deadly animal and gave it a calm look.

The creature quietly stared at her, then its nose rose into the air and it took in a long breath and gave what almost sounded like a sigh.

Charli looked over her shoulder at Fred, whom she wasn't happy with. "Now, sit. No more shooting." Fred planted his butt on a stump, looking like a scolded puppy. She turned back to the bear, also sitting. She noted the fur on its back leg was slick and shiny. She couldn't tell from here, but hopefully the bullet had missed the bear's artery and there wasn't too much bleeding.

She slowly approached the injured animal with her hands out in front of her in a nonthreatening manner. "It's okay, Mr. Bear. I just want to look at your wound. I won't hurt you." The bear lowered his head and laid it on his paws on the ground. Charli hadn't expected that, but she'd take it. Until she could physically touch him, she couldn't

2

really "talk" to him, not with her mind. That's how her gift worked. If she wanted to communicate mentally with an animal, she had to be in physical contact.

Crouching as close as she could safely get to the site of the wound, Charli could see the injury wasn't fatal, but the bullet did need to be surgically removed. She didn't have those tools with her. She was supposed to be here to verify that Fred and Jed had caught a bear and to take its measurements for the records, and make sure it was dead. So much for needing to check the latter.

She heaved a sigh. "Fred, any ideas how to get this creature back into the trailer so I can take him to the clinic for minor surgery?"

"Shoot, Doc. You'd need a tranq gun."

She hadn't brought one since she hadn't planned on taking a bear home with her. The animal gave a grunt and pushed onto all fours. Charli quickly stepped back and Fred readied his rifle. The bear turned, and to everyone's amazement, loaded himself into the back of the horse trailer and lay down.

"Huh," Jed snorted from where he lay panting on the grass. "Butter my butt and call me a biscuit. How'd he know to do that?"

What puzzled Charli more was how these two yokels captured the beast in the first place. "So, Fred, how did you and Jed get a live bear?"

Fred glanced at Jed, then smiled at her right nicely. "Well, Jed 'n me had been tracking this monster all mornin'." Charli raised her brow, but kept silent. This should be good. "He shor was one sneaky bastard, yes'm. We cornered him up on the ridge north a here, then he jumped from behind bushes an' attacked us—"

Jed ran up and threw a fist in the air. "Yeah, I punched him in the face—"

"Wait," Charli scrunched her brows, "you punched the bear, or Fred?"

Jed popped his hand onto his hip. "For bein' a doc and all, Doc, you can be slow as molasses in winter."

She smiled. "You're right, Jed. Of course, you got right up into the bear's face and punched him. Probably saved Fred, too, right?"

Jed's eyes popped wide. "Yeah"—he turned to his brother—"I saved your ass."

Fred jumped to his feet. "You did not. I saved yours." *Wait for it.* "I found the tree we climbed to get away."

And there it was. Charli had all the story she needed, except how the bear had become unconscious. "Okay, guys. How did you knock out the bear to load him?"

"Oh," Fred said as his cheeks blushed crimson. "When the tree went over the edge of the steep bankside, it dumped us in the crick and caused a rockslide the bear fell with. We had to dig him out first."

"Then I punched him in the face," Jed added.

Fred shoved his brother. "Stop tall tellin'." Charli walked toward her truck to bring it around and hook up the trailer. The boys kept arguing as she went. "We're busted already. Quit jawin'—"

"You started it . . ."

Charli just shook her head. Such was life in Shedford, Oregon.

CHAPTER TWO

C harli watched the truck's side mirrors as she backed the horse trailer with her patient to the large stalls at the back of her clinic reserved for horses and cows. She had laid hay on an old horse pad to soften the stall's cold concrete. With the bear's thick fur, none of that was really needed, but her love for creatures big and small wouldn't let her do anything less.

Back inside the building, she stepped into the aisle separating stalls and leaned the pitchfork against the wall. She didn't want something to happen and have the bear end up injured more by falling on the three tines.

Opening the trailer's gate, Charli looked around it to see what the lying bear would do. He'd gotten in on his own. Would he come out also? From his prone position on the metal floor, one black eyeball looked up at her, then closed. Guess that was a no.

Sighing, she shuffled through the stall toward the interior hallway. There were a couple of steaks in the fridge she could use to wrap medication in to lure him into the stall and knock him out so she could pull the bullet from his hindquarter. Then a big—no, huge—cup of coffee would be called for. She'd be lucky to get to the office in time for the morning meeting. Being late was not part of her style, but the animals came first.

Oh shit. She'd forgotten to close the stall's back gate, leaving the bear loose if he decided to get up. She spun around and slammed into a broad, naked, muscular chest. Her defensive training kicked in and she spun him and pinned him to the floor in two seconds flat.

She pulled his arm farther back, bringing the shoulder socket close to popping out. "Who are you and why are you in my barn?" She hadn't asked the most important question: Why was he naked? Because, hot damn, he looked good enough to eat. Not to mention he smelled divine. Musky and woodsy.

He jerked under her. "Shit, lady. I don't know who you are or where I am. I woke and saw someone walk out of the stall. Did you bring me here?"

Charli eased up her hold. "No, I didn't bring you here. And you weren't in the stall. I put hay down in an empty pen. So tell me the truth." She yanked on his arm.

"Oww, fuck, lady." He bucked hard, but she held on. "Get off me."

"Not until you tell me who you are and why you're here."

"I just told you. I don't know who I am."

Whoa, he hadn't said that. "How can you not know who you are?" She jumped off his back and reached for the pitchfork along the wall.

He slowly rolled to sit up. He must've realized then he was naked; his face flooded red and his hands quickly covered his junk. From the little she saw, he had nothing to be ashamed of. Her mouth suddenly felt dry. She pushed all that business aside. Now wasn't the moment to think of the last time she'd had sex—she couldn't remember when, anyway.

She raised onto tiptoes and peeked over the gate to the stall. Damn, the bear was gone. Shit, shit, shit. Maybe he wouldn't go far and she could find him and take care of his injury before it became infected.

If the animal died because this asshole took her attention, she'd put a bullet in the guy's ass and push him out the door.

After pivoting his front side away from her, he ran fingers through his soft brown hair. "Look, lady . . ." Dark circles marred the skin under his eyes. "I have a hell of a headache and . . . do you have anything I can put on? Shorts or sweats?"

"I have a lab coat in the office, but I'm not leaving you here by yourself while I get it." She waved the pitchfork to make sure he knew she had it.

He rubbed his hands over his face. "Let's go." He stood, keeping his front side turned away. Which was fine with her. His backside looked pretty damn nice, also. She wondered how he kept in such good shape. He wasn't a spring chicken. Probably her age, lower thirties. She noted a tattoo on his bicep, but couldn't tell what it was from her distance.

As they walked up the hall, he kept his hands in front, probably covering himself. She smiled, thinking what his reaction would be if she made him put his hands behind his head. Shit, tingles started in her lower belly; something she hadn't felt in a long time.

Her prisoner stopped and took a deep breath. His head tipped back and a growly groan escaped his throat. "Lady, you can't—" His tongue swiped across his lips.

She waited for him to continue and when he didn't, she prodded. "Can't what?"

He turned his head enough for her to see his profile. Again, perfect. Straight nose, strong jawline, high cheekbones. Her tongue wanted to glide over his day-old whiskers, wanted to feel their roughness. Her heat pooled lower.

The man gasped, throwing a hand against the wall, tightening it into a fist. "That, woman. You can't do that."

Charli frowned and jabbed the pitchfork at him. "Keep walking, dude." What did he mean? He couldn't read her mind, could he? After accepting a position with the pack fellowship, she'd learned an entire species had been living side by side with humans that few knew about. And she understood why their secret needed to be kept. If the world knew supernatural beings existed, everything would go to hell in a handbasket really damn quick.

She directed him to her clinic office, where a white coat hung on the wall next to the door. He slipped it on and realized it was barely long enough to cover what needed covering. He took it off and wrapped the sleeves around his waist, tying them at his back. His hands felt where the coat lay against the sides of his thick thighs and he smiled. "Well, looks like you get to keep your view, at least."

She gasped and her entire body burst with embarrassed heat. Of course, she enjoyed her "view," but she sure as hell wasn't letting him know that. Trying to cover her shame with an indignant expression, she pushed him forward. "Get inside and shut up."

He exploded into a deep laugh that rolled over her with longing. Shit, that was so not good. Why was this stranger having such an effect on her? She'd been around good-looking men before and hadn't felt the need to hump their leg. *Fuck.*

He opened the door and she pushed in behind him toward her desk. "Sit down and be quiet." Charli took a key from her desk and opened a small drawer to the side. She pulled out a gun, then set the pitchfork behind her. After gingerly rolling her chair from the desk, she sat and laid the gun close to her.

She smiled. "So, we were discussing why you're naked . . . I mean, why you're here." She shook her head. "Forget the naked—of course, being naked is part— I mean, I need to know . . . you're, you're naked." Shit. She shut her mouth before she could say something worse.

CHAPTER THREE

He burst into laughter watching the beautiful woman on the other side of the desk flounder with her words. Fuck, she was stunning. *Mine.* Where had that come from? He glanced at her face and the word sprang into his mind again. *Mine!*

What in the world? He couldn't understand this primal need to take her, tear her clothes off, and slide into her, claiming her as his own. Fucking hell, she smelled unbelievably delicious. More than anything, he wanted to snuggle his face into her pussy and lap at her hot center. He dropped his hand onto his lap as the coat started to rise in the center. He shifted to one ass cheek and crossed a leg over the other.

Now wasn't the time to get hot and bothered. He had more important things to figure out, like his name, for starters. He'd have her later.

She flipped her long, honey-colored hair over her shoulder. "Let's start over, shall we? My name is Charlynne Avers—Charli, preferably. And you?"

He racked his brain for everything he could recall, which was alarmingly little. He dropped his look to his hands. "I . . . don't know. In fact, I don't remember much."

Charli's expression was a mix of concern and disbelief. "Okay, tell me what you do remember."

He sighed and stared out the window at the yellow-and-brown field leading to the snowcapped mountain in the distance. Beautiful. Something else he didn't remember. "I was . . . dreaming a very weird dream, woke up with a very bad headache in a horse trailer in the back of your stall, then found myself on the ground with my face shoved into the concrete."

Charli rolled her eyes. "In my defense, you scared the crap out of me. People don't sneak in the back door without a reason."

"Yeah, my reason being I didn't know where I was, or why, or who you were."

Her eyes narrowed and her sexy lips flattened into a straight line. "What were you dreaming about?"

She would ask that question. If he told her he'd dreamed he was a bear, she'd put him in an insane asylum, or shoot him on the spot as a deranged loony. "I dreamed I was chasing a guy, when out of nowhere, something sharp stung me in my leg and as I was falling under, I saw the most beautiful woman I'd ever seen." His hand slid from his waist to his thigh, feeling for an injury that wasn't there. "When I woke up, I found myself looking at a stack of hay and you walking away."

Her brow raised. "That's it?"

"That's it." He cleared his throat. He'd love something to drink but wouldn't ask her. He had bigger problems than feeling thirsty. There was this primal need to touch the woman and something strange going on with his body. He didn't even know how to explain it to himself, much less someone he didn't know.

She blinked her beautiful long lashes and glanced down, her gaze sweeping over him like a hot caress. Fuck, he wanted to grab her and kiss her like nothing else mattered. "What about before?"

"Before what?"

She sighed with exasperation. He wasn't trying to be difficult, really. But she was hot enough to melt steel. At that moment, she was adorable as she rolled her eyes. "When you woke in the stall, did you see a bear? My bear is missing and injured."

"A bear? You had a bear in the horse trailer? Are you sure?" He didn't like the way this conversation was going. There was a bear, then there was him. And he wasn't a bear. He had hands, for crying out loud. His entire body tensed as if it knew something he didn't.

She clenched her teeth and glared at him. "Yes, I know what a bear is. I've been a vet here in the mountains for several years."

"Oh, this is a vet's office?" That made sense, especially now that he saw the framed degrees hanging on the wall behind her, including one for veterinary forensic sciences. Brainy and beautiful. And his. His? There was something wrong with him.

Her face flushed and she glanced around the room as if trying to see it from his point of view. "It's not really an *office* office. I usually don't work with small animals like cats or dogs. I work mostly with farmers' livestock and bigger animals. So I'm on location mostly. Occasionally a horse or cow will come in. I keep them in the stalls you're familiar with here."

Her words caught his attention. There was a massive emptiness in his brain. "Where is *here*, exactly, besides your non-office office?"

Her delay in answering brought his eyes to hers. She leaned back in her chair, arms crossed, chewing on her plump red lip. He would like to have that piece of flesh in his mouth, too. He felt the coat covering his lap rise again. He shifted in his chair.

Charli sat forward, elbows on the desk. "Okay, I'll bite. *Here* is southwestern Oregon, not far from the California border."

"Oregon?" He didn't know why, but he wasn't expecting that answer.

Her brows rose and she gave him a curious glance. "Where did you think we were?"

"I'm not sure. But the East Coast came to mind." At that moment, his situation sank in. He had no identity, no family, nowhere to go, and his mind kept saying he was a fucking bear. He dropped his head into his hands and pulled on his hair—just a little pain to prove to himself he was alive. This wasn't a dream. His stomach gurgled loudly.

"I'm taking a guess here," Charli said. He heard a smile in her voice and looked at her sparkling eyes. "But I bet you don't remember when you last ate." Her smile blew him away. Laughter bubbled out of him, partially from her humor, partially to keep from breaking down. It was surreal. He had no idea of anything in his life and the world at the moment, but being near this woman kept him from losing his shit. Her smile, her scent, her eyes, they all kept him grounded and able to try to figure out what was going on.

She laid her arm across the desk and held her hand open to him. "I'm going on a hunch and trying something I've never done before." He looked from her palm to her face. She wiggled her fingers. "Give me your hand."

This was weird. Then again, maybe it wasn't. What did he know? Squat. He laid his open hand on hers. Instantly, sweat popped out on his forehead and a cold shiver ran down his back. Joyous energy spread outward from his heart, lifting the gloom of his situation, taking away his worry, filling him with happiness. *Mate.* Mate? What the fuck did that mean? And who said it?

He knew Charli felt the same way. Not only by the mixed expressions on her face, but also because he felt her heart. Then he *felt* her in his mind, but only part of it. She was searching for something.

Hello?

Yes, mate. Waiting. Always for you.

She didn't reply. He couldn't ignore what just happened. He snatched his hand from hers and backed against the wall. "Who the fuck was talking in my head without me?"

She looked astounded. "You really don't know, don't remember, do you?"

"Don't know or remember what?" His body fought an invisible pull for control. A low rumble sounded in his chest. He tried so hard to make a memory, any memory, come to him. Nothing. His pulse pounded in his ears. He couldn't catch his breath. Out. He had to get out of the room.

Charli stood from her chair. "Barry, calm down. Barry. Look at me."

He snapped his eyes to hers. "My name is Barry? Seriously?" Damn, if that wasn't a corny name. He'd prefer a manlier one. She smiled.

"I doubt it, but since I know who half of you is, Barry is appropriate." *Half of me?* What the hell? She held out her hand to him again. This time he was more hesitant. Maybe she was a bit kooky herself. She snagged his hand and opened the door. "Stop being a sissy and come on."

"Sissy? Me? I wasn't the one saying things in my head." What did he just say? She laughed. Damned if the sound didn't make him happy.

She tugged him into the house. Even though he was chilled from the reality of his situation, her holding his hand warmed him to the marrow. "Let's get you clothes and breakfast. Then we can figure out what to do with you."

He liked the sound of that. And boy did he like the feel of her hand in his. If he had his way, he'd keep it there forever. *Mine. Always mine.* Shit. He didn't know where the thoughts were coming from or why he fought this dominant side trying to control him.

CHAPTER FOUR

In her kitchen, Charli chopped the last of the chives and tossed them in the pan with the eggs, tomatoes, and spinach. Coffee would be ready soon. The seventeen-inch TV under the far cabinet aired the local morning news with weather and traffic every twenty minutes. Not that traffic in Shedford was bad, but having another voice in the house made her feel less lonely.

Her mind wouldn't stop returning to the gorgeous man she'd found in her horse stall. Obviously, he was a shifter, but the entity she'd encountered wasn't like other animals she'd communicated with. When she made contact with his bear, she knew Barry wasn't a bad guy, or wouldn't hurt her, at least. The bear would make sure of that. She felt a strong bond she'd never had with wildlife. Charli didn't really know how to explain to a shifter that he was one. As far as she knew, they were all aware of their animals, so this was not only unusual, but difficult to figure out.

She had never tried talking to a shifter's animal while he was in human form until that morning. The thought had never occurred to her in the short time she'd known of their existence. She needed to compare the difference the next time she was with Devin or Russel. Maybe Barry's animal was perfectly normal for a shifter.

Her ear caught the anchorwoman talking about the jewelry store heist a couple of weeks ago. Not only was neither the thief nor the loot found, but the police had no theories on how the burglar got in and out without tripping the sophisticated alarm system. Similar to a bank robbery a month ago where the vault was entered and no one had any idea how the perp got in or out.

Barry walked in from the bathroom where he had put on the clothes she handed him. He was a big guy . . . everywhere. He filled out her biggest pair of sweatpants quite nicely, except the legs stopped above his ankles. But honestly, her eyes didn't get that far down. Her XL T-shirt would barely go over his head. It draped over his well-muscled shoulders. Damn, damn, damn. She knew what she wanted for breakfast.

Barry's head snapped up. His eyes flashed between gold and his normal hazel and drilled into hers. He stalked toward her with aggressive steps, pushing her against the refrigerator. His nose ran up the side of her neck. Chills raced down her arms.

She should be afraid of this stranger cornering her, threatening her wellbeing. But her body screamed the opposite. It wanted to take this man to the floor and sit on his face until he learned to breathe through his ears.

Fortunately, or not, her brain overruled, bringing everything to a screeching halt.

His chest vibrated against hers. "I told you, you can't do that. You smell so good. I can't control it. I—I lose myself."

Well, yippy-ki-yay. The bear part of him she'd spoken to in the clinic was right. He'd decided she was his mate. When she got to the office, she needed to have a long talk with one of the shifters about mate stuff. And could it be turned off?

She couldn't deny the physical attraction between them. Shit. Their chemistry was off the friggin' chart. But she was human, and her heart didn't fall instantly in love because someone called her mate. Though her heart was already doing flip-flops every time he met her gaze. She could see how easily it would be to fall for a big guy like him. Those eyes, that face, and oh, good lord, that body. It was impossible to ignore her hormones bouncing for his attention.

Charli pushed Barry back, hurried to the stove, and flipped the omelet before it burned. She called over her shoulder without looking back, "How about you put toast in. I want two pieces. Butter is in the fridge door, at the top. Jelly, too." While he rustled around the kitchen, she calmed herself and clamped down on her emotions.

The little she did know about shifters included that they could smell a hot babe from five streets over. According to the two single males she worked with at the fellowship, anyway. She'd swear they were horn dogs if she didn't already know what they were. Her knowledge about shifters was very much limited to the masculine side. Not to mention they were half *human* male, which made it worse. But she liked the guys and was glad they worked together.

After making her plate, she shoveled the rest onto Barry's, figuring he ate like the guys from the office. And she was right. His plate was half empty before she got to her first piece of toast.

For conversation's sake, she thought she should ask him about his life, but she realized that would've been a short story. She snorted. Barry looked up at her.

"What's so funny?" He gave her another of those panty-melting smiles, and her appetite for food was replaced with a different one.

"Just me, being a dimwit." Being around a hot guy was messing with her mind. She wasn't used to having one in her house.

He nodded and tilted his head toward his plate. "Do you have any idea why I lost my memory? Was I in a car accident or something where I hit my head?"

She doubted it. Shifters were known for being strong, so whatever happened had really hit him hard. "From what Fred and Jed said, the bear went down with the rockslide and was buried. My guess is your head got banged around quite a bit."

His eyes widened and he stared at her. "Wait a second. How are a bear and my head related? Did we both fall?"

Maybe this would be a good time to bring up this shifter thing with him. "Say, Barry. You know what a shifter is?"

He gave her a confused look. Poor guy. "You're probably not talking about someone who works shift hours, are you?"

"Why would you say that? Do you remember something from your past?" It could be so helpful. Especially seeing she had no idea what to do with him. The guy had no memory. Not to mention she was incredibly tempted to keep him. Even if it was to stare at his gorgeous face. Right. Okay, and maybe do some really dirty things to him.

"Sorta. From my past *two* hours, I've learned nothing with you will be normal." His sincere smile warmed her heart. "So I'm expecting a wild ride."

Oh yes. A wild ride would just be the beginning. She'd ride him all night long and then let him do whatever he wanted with her. Remembering what her emotions caused, she sucked in a sharp breath and pointed at Barry, who breathed deeply across the table.

"Sit still, dude. That was my fault, but you need to control yourself. That's part of being a shifter." Sure, get him to feel guilty over her inability to stop her lustful thoughts.

His head tilted and eyes narrowed. "So you're telling me I'm a shifter, which is what, exactly?"

Great. How was she to convince someone they were part animal? Usually it was the shifter trying to convince the human.

She set her fork down. "Okay, there's no beating around the bush here. You were born with two souls. One is human and the other is ursine or bear." She stared at his stoic face, unable to tear her eyes away from his gold-rimmed irises. Suddenly he threw his head back and guffawed, slapping the table with his hand. The orange juice in her glass rippled.

Barry collected his dishes and strolled to the sink. "You're a funny woman, Charli. I like you." He washed his plate and rinsed the glass. "Next, you're going to tell me I can *turn into* a bear during a full moon."

"A full moon has nothing to do with it. As I understand, it's based on want. If you *want* to shift." She watched him closely, worried how he'd take the idea.

He rested his palms on the edge of the sink and stared out the window. The view from the kitchen was her favorite in all the house. A lake big enough for taking out a paddle boat stretched beyond the flat plain of evergreens, to rocky hills, then the mountains in the distance.

Most of the town was nestled between several mountain ranges. In the countryside here, she found peace like no other place she'd been. Right now, she hoped that peace found Barry.

Without moving from the window, he spoke. "In my dream, the first thing I remember thinking was that I was in my animal form—my other half. The thought angered me. I felt a rage build toward that other half. The bear went berserk and attacked the first person it saw, which happened to be some skinny guy wearing camo overalls."

Charli remembered Jed had on camouflage clothing. As did Fred, but he was standing on the tractor laughing his ass off at Jed.

"Then you came into sight, and the fury burning inside vanished. I wasn't lost anymore. I felt whole. There weren't two parts of me when I looked at you. You completed me."

Tears came to Charli's eyes. Men didn't say things like that to her. Ever. Maybe it was that this man with no past and the ability to start fresh was telling her that she'd given him something when he felt lost. If she found out later that he'd seen *Jerry Maguire*, she'd so kick his ass into next week for making her all mushy. But for now . . .

Barry's head bent for a moment before he continued. "So when you say there's another half to me, I fully believe you. But I will never,

ever believe I was born this way." He turned to face her. "I know in my heart, I was born human, one soul."

Charli sat stunned. She had no words to comfort him, no way to tell him if he was right or wrong. He really needed Devin and Russel to talk with him. They could help and answer his questions. "I'm going to take you over to visit some friends. They'll be able to help us out."

The gorgeous man dipped his head with a sigh and ran his fingers through his hair. Then he looked up with a sly grin. "So, have I convinced you to have sex with me yet?"

CHAPTER FIVE

C harli held tightly to Barry's elbow as she rushed them up the steps to the pack fellowship's office. She was a few minutes late, but she had a darn good reason. And it wasn't sex. She was not *that* easy. Men.

They entered the main area, where partitioned desks lined the long sides of the room. A few of the people in the office gave Barry a curious look, but Charli's frown had them turning back to mind their business. At the far end sat Director Scott Milkan's office—the big kahuna. The wall opposite his side was covered by whiteboards with unreadable writing; corkboards with newspaper clippings, notes, recipes, the phone number to the pizza delivery joint, and everything else that could be pinned to it; and taped-up crime scene photos.

Charli plopped Barry at her "office" partition and told him to wait until the meeting was over. She didn't know what else to do with him. Besides, he needed to talk with Devin and Russel.

Opening the door to Director Milkan's office, she gave a guilty grin, said good morning to the four gathered around the table and took a seat. A box of donuts sat in the middle of the table. Looked like she wasn't the only late one today. She didn't make a habit of having break-fast twice, but there was a first time for everything and those donuts were calling her name.

"All right," Director Milkan began, "now that we're all here, let's get started." He turned to the lady sitting beside him. She was pretty, with thick auburn hair falling around her shoulders. "This is Detective Tamara Gibbons with Shedford City Police. She has a case she'd like our help with."

The director cast his attention to Charli. "This is Agent Charlynne Avers. Charli, to us. She's our in-house animal expert and longtime veterinarian for the area. She's also what we call a critter whisperer."

Detective Gibbons gave her a worried expression. Charli smiled. "I can communicate with animals better than ninety-nine percent of the world, that's all." From the detective's new expression, that explanation didn't help much.

Director Milkan gave a chin pop toward the guy sitting next to Charli. "This is Agent Devin Sonder. He's a panther shifter and left his detective position with the LAPD to join our new fellowship." Devin did his usual single nod, then wove his fingers together, resting his hands on the table.

Devin was a curious one to her. She hadn't figured him out yet. Truthfully, their team of four was so new, they were still working on group dynamics and becoming productive coworkers. She itched to talk with Devin's panther to get the inside scoop on the human, but that would be rude and a bit biased. It would be like asking his big sister what she thought of her bratty little brother.

He was always calm and cool. Little seemed to bother him. But she imagined years with the LAPD had taught the agents to be the strong, silent type or risk being put in an insane asylum. He was also very hand-some—the high school quarterback all the girls crushed on. Not her type, but she liked his dry sense of humor.

Next to Devin sat the fourth member of their group. She glanced at Russel and almost spit out her mouthful of coffee. Hot liquid out the nose would not be good right now. He was practically drooling over the police detective. Devin nudged Russel with an elbow and Russel closed his mouth.

Director Milkan continued introducing the team. "And this is Agent Russel Mayer. We call him Sinatra."

Detective Gibbons turned to Milkan. "Why Sinatra, does he sing?"

Russel grinned. "Yeah, baby. I'll sing for you anytime."

Gibbons slowly turned her head to face Russel. Holy shit. She was going to tear him a new asshole. Her shit-eating grin matched his. "Thank you, Agent Mayer. Wednesday night, Junior's Bar, bring your best karaoke. I will drill you into the ground."

Woo-hoo. Russel had met his match. Go girlfriend! Charli *had* to become friends with this woman. Devin covered his smile with his hand. "Actually, Russel is a—" He looked at Russel. "What are you naturally?"

"Eh, you know, whatever the occasion calls for," Russel added as he sat straighter in his chair.

The detective's eyes grew wide. "I had no idea . . ." Gibbons said. "How does him being a multishifter relate to Frank Sinatra?"

He gave a haughty smirk and leaned closer to her. "It's my ol' blue eyes, baby."

Gibbons rolled her eyes. "Got it. Sinatra was called Ol' Blue Eyes."

"Mayer." Director Milkan gave him a stern look.

Russel sighed. "Actually, it's from my former department. Several of us hung out after our shift and we were dubbed the Rat Pack. And each of us got a name. Mine was Sinatra."

Milkan shook his head. "Detective Gibbons, please continue with the case."

"Thank you, Director." Gibbons opened a file folder and slid it toward the others. "About a month ago, the local bank was robbed.

The perpetrator got away with several hundred thousand in cash and gold."

Charli nodded. "I remember that happening. Did they catch the guy?"

"Unfortunately," Gibbons began, "we haven't." Charli noted the detective's use of "we." She needed to remember she was now part of the "we." Gibbons pulled out a second folder and copied her previous actions. "Two weeks ago, a high-end jewelry store was robbed." Charli remembered that, too, but wasn't commenting this time. "And we had the same scenario and unexplained happenings as at the bank."

Devin asked, "What scenario and unexplained happenings?"

"That's what brings me to you guys." She glanced at Director Milkan. "The chief told me, privately, what your group . . . uh . . . that you people . . ." She seemed to have problems finding the words to describe them. Director Milkan smiled and patted her hand.

"No worries, Detective. Our Fellowship of Packs United is our means of policing the paranormal society to keep the peace between humans and paras. Our goal is to protect as well as keep our presence unknown."

Gibbons stiffened. "But I know about you. So does the chief."

Milkan smiled anew. "We understand that to do our job effectively, we need help from the human side of the population. Not only have we assembled a team from various packs and species, we want to work hand in hand with humans, for our issues cross into each other's worlds continually. We must work together, which means those who need to know about us are informed. Obviously, the chief trusts you with secrecy and believes you able to work with others."

Gibbons coughed into her hand and smiled. "I think it's more like the chief slipped up and mentioned you guys, and I wouldn't believe him. I owe him twenty bucks and a pizza now." Charli and everyone else laughed at her confession. The tension squeezing the group at the table was gone.

"Now"—Milkan continued—"back to the cases."

Detective Gibbons looked at the files in the center. "Right. We are completely unable to understand how these two operations were carried out. The MO was the same. The burglar came in during the night, stole the goods without setting off any alarms, and disappeared."

"That seems normal," Devin said.

"The part that has us stumped is there is no evidence of entry or exit, or DNA left on-site. The only way we can tell a robbery happened is the missing merchandise and video footage."

Charli leaned forward. "Wait, you have video evidence and still can't find anything?"

Gibbons frowned. "If we didn't have the exact same burglar in both locations, we wouldn't have known what to think about the video. The tape shows the thief is a naked woman."

Russel cleared his throat and took on a serious face. "Boss, if you'd like me to study the footage for clues, I'd happily take on that challenge for the team."

Everyone groaned, including the visiting detective. A smile burst onto Russel's face. "What? You gotta admit that was a good one, though, right? I mean, she set it up perfectly."

"Mayer"—Director Milkan started—"you are the biggest walking sexual harassment case I've ever seen."

"Aww, Boss," Russel laid a hand over his heart, "I didn't know you cared that much."

"I don't," he barked. "Now can it before I throw you in the can."

Russel's face lit up. "Tamara, here, can handcuff me if she wants." He growled and swiped his hand like a paw.

In a blink of an eye, Detective Gibbons stood behind Russel, one of her cuffs around his wrist and the other hooked around his chair's arm. He pulled on the metal. "Uh, yeah, this isn't what I meant, but it's a start." He winked at her, but she ignored him.

"As I was saying," Gibbons said, "we have the perp on tape but have no idea how she gets in or out or what happens to the stolen goods. The chief was hoping maybe you guys had some insight."

Director Milkan slid the files toward Devin. "Sonder, this is yours. Let me know what you find out."

Devin scooped up the files. "Yes, sir."

Director Milkan stood, signaling the meeting was over. "Detective, e-mail footage and whatever else you have to Devin. Be sure to get his info before you leave." He offered his hand to the woman and she accepted it.

"It'll be great working with your team, Director." She raised a brow. "Most of the team, anyway." Everyone headed for the door except Russel, who made a commotion behind them.

"Hey, wait! I'm still cuffed to the chair." They all kept walking. "You can't leave me like this, you scrubs." Milkan closed his office door after he walked out.

CHAPTER SIX

After a good laugh on Russel's behalf, Detective Tamara Gibbons got her cuffs back and left with a smile on her face, opposed to the grimace she'd had earlier. Now, Charli had her problem to deal with.

"Director Milkan," Charli called out. The director held his hand up, as if saying 'not now.'

Milkan opened the door to his office and stepped in.

"Wait, Director Milkan." Standing in the doorway, he turned toward Charli. She waved Barry to come over.

Suddenly, Charli felt herself jerked into the director's office, the door slamming in front of her. Milkan pulled her to his face. Her head spun from the furious movements. Charli was ready to shit her pants. He growled at her. "What is that man doing here? How do you know him?"

Charli's mouth moved, but no words came out. This was too out of character for her boss. "He's why I need to talk with you, sir." He didn't move. Now she was getting pissed. "You're hurting my arm, Milkan."

He jerked his hand back and came out of the daze he seemed to be in. "Shit. I apologize, Avers." His hand snaked to the back of her head and he pulled her in, smashing her nose to his sternum. He let out a sigh. "My sister was attacked in her office by a stranger. And ever since, I've been . . . overprotective of the females I work with."

"Not a problem, sir," Charli mumbled against his tie. "I'd just like to breathe." He stepped back, again apologizing. She rubbed her nose, scrunched it up a few times, then was back to normal. "Sorry to hear about your sister, sir."

He brushed it off and headed for his desk. "That was a while ago. I think I was more traumatized about it than she was." Charli reached for the door to let Barry in. "Stop." She stared at him, wondering *what the hell*. "I'd prefer not to have civilians in my office. Who knows what they might read on my desk or overhear. You can understand that?"

She did. But still, she was a bit creeped out. Probably because they really didn't know each other's idiosyncrasies. And bosses always seem overstressed. "Yes, sir."

"Come on, Charli. No 'sir' for me. Treat me like one of the guys." He smiled at her.

"If that's what you want, I'll tape your drawers shut, put Vaseline on the handles, and pull one of the wheels off your chair."

He let out a burst of laughter, making her feel more comfortable. She quickly stuck her head out the door before Milkan stopped laughing and told Barry to wait again. Charli stood in front of his desk. "Si— Milkan"—they both smiled at her catching herself—"I've had an interesting morning and I need your advice on what to do."

He gestured to the table they'd sat around earlier. "Pull up a chair, Charli. Tell me what's happened."

Once she was comfortably seated, she continued. "This morning, through strange circumstances, I found a shifter with no memory. He doesn't even remember his name or that he's a shifter."

"That's the man outside?"

"Yes, s— Yes." Her mama raised her right, and it would take time before she could break the rules. "I don't know what to do with him, but I think he needs to talk with other shifters to figure out what he truly is."

He seemed to relax a bit. She knew Barry posed no threat, and hopefully her boss did, too. "I see. I agree that he should stay here and talk to the men for a while." He stood and grabbed his car keys off the desk. "You did right bringing him here, Charli. Now, I have an errand I need—" The receptionist buzzed his intercom. "Sir, the mayor is on line one for you. He doesn't sound happy."

Her boss cursed under his breath. "Thank you, Sally." He looked at Charli. "If you'll excuse me, I need to take this call. We'll continue later." Charli turned for the door. "Oh, and Charli, keep me updated on his memory. Let me know right away when it comes back." He pushed a button on his phone, not letting Charli reply. She hurried out.

Barry paced in front of a couple empty desks. He gave her a concerned look. "What happened in there?"

"Well"—she started—"several things, really. Mainly learning how to work with my new boss, getting to know his personalities and . . . tendencies."

"Anything about me?"

"Sorry, Barry. The mayor called and we had to cut it short." She looked at Sonder and Mayer. "Come with me." She took his hand and led him to Sonder's perfectly clean and organized desk. She could see him being a bit OCD about having everything in its place. Note to self: Don't even borrow a pen from him. You'll mess up his desk.

"Guys, I'd like you to meet Barry." She gestured to the man standing beside her. "Barry, this is Sonder and Sinatra. I mean, Mayer." She flashed Russel an apologetic look.

"Sinatra?" Barry said.

"Long story," Charli said. "I'll tell you later. Right now, we need to decide what to do with you."

Sonder leaned against the partition separating the desks. "What do you mean by that?"

Barry answered before she did. "Seems I have amnesia. Don't remember anything. Not even that I'm a shifter."

"Seriously?" Mayer said, shock clear in his voice and his wide eyes. "You can forget you're a shifter? Bet that came as a hell of a surprise."

"No kidding. Anyway, guys, we need help on what to do next. I've never dealt with something like this."

"I've seen it before," Devin said. She imagined he'd seen *everything*, working in LA. "Best plan is to get your memory back before much else."

"How do we do that?" Charli asked.

"Go back to the scene of the crime. Look around where you were found to get clues why you were there and what you were doing."

Charli pulled her phone from her back pocket. "Perfect idea. Thank you so much, Sonder." She twirled around and headed for her desk. Once there, she noticed Barry staring at her, a curious look in his eyes.

She raised her brows. "What's wrong?"

"I just wondered about something."

She nodded. "What?"

"Your . . . specialty. Were you born with this ability?"

Ah, the talking-to-animals conversation. She sat down across from him, meeting his gaze. "I think so. Mom told me stories about my antics when I was really young. She had laid me on a blanket on the wood floor in the living room. After babbling to our lap dog, it grabbed the blanket's edge and dragged me around the floor while I giggled and gurgled." She smiled, remembering her mother's stories and how much fun it had been to hear them.

Barry leaned back in his seat, arms crossed. "Your mom thought you told the dog to do that?"

"It took her a while before she really believed I could talk to animals. I thought everyone could do it when I was little. I remember getting strange looks when talking to random animals at the beach and park. I told one guy that his dog was really sick and needed to go to the doctor. The dog looked fine.

"Later on, he came to the playground to thank me for telling him. Turns out the dog had liver cancer in an early stage and they were able to operate to remove it all."

Barry gazed at her with pride. "Amazing. Is that why you're part of this special fellowship?"

She shrugged. "I'm guessing so. How they found out I could do that is beyond me. We just got started as a department. We really haven't had a case yet. These robberies are the first things the police have brought to us." She snorted. "Hell, I haven't even had the right kind of training to allow me to be in the field with the others. I mean, I took some training, but the big stuff—I have to go to Virginia for it, and since the team is so new, we haven't had a chance.

"My ability is all they cared about, and while I love to help, I feel like things are moving way too slowly for me to learn how to handle these cases properly. They are still making plans for training at Quantico." She pursed her lips. "I feel like if I'd had the right training, this whole thing could have been handled better. I would have known the right way to approach my job."

They were quiet for a moment. She remembered what she'd been about to do before and pulled her cell phone out of her pocket.

Barry frowned. "Who are you calling?"

"Our ol' buddies, Fred and Jed."

CHAPTER SEVEN

W hat in the hell were you doing out here?" In her SUV, Charli carefully followed the beat-up Chevy leading them along the narrow gravel road winding the steep hill. "I haven't seen a house in miles."

Barry shrugged. "Hopefully, I'll be able to tell you soon."

She glanced at him, then back to the narrow rock road. What if, after he got his memory back, he left her? Would she ever see him again? See his beautiful smile or hear the timbre in his voice that sent shivers racing through her? A tinge of sadness touched her heart, bringing tears to the surface.

Hang on a goddamned second. What the hell was wrong with her? She met this guy six hours ago, and she can't live without him now? She had to be coming up on her time of the month because she wasn't this much of a sucker for any man. She hardened herself, swallowed the tears. He would leave when the time came. A guy that gorgeous must have a wife and family somewhere. She peeked at his left hand on his knee. No ring. *Well, duh, shifters can't wear that kind of stuff for obvious reasons.* She bonked her palm on her forehead.

Barry laughed at her. "Do you have conversations with yourself in your head all the time? I have to say, it can be comical to someone watching."

She'd never thought of it that way. "I do. All the time, I guess. How strange. I bet it's because of how I communicate with animals. They talk to me silently in my head."

He turned to her. "That is fascinating. I've never met anyone who could do that." Charli looked at him with a *do you know what you just said* expression. He laughed deeply and honestly. "Not that I'd remember if I *had* met anyone, right?"

The Chevy truck in front of her pulled to the side. Finally. They were seriously in BFE. Everyone piled out of the vehicles and looked around.

Fred pointed toward the edge of the road where a cliff dropped off to the water below. "That, thar, is the tree—was the tree—we climbed." A huge hole dug out of the side of the cliff's face had dangling roots that looked torn at the ends. "Careful crossin' the road. I almost got runned over this mornin'."

They shimmied over to peer at the base of the cliff. Piles of small boulders and rock debris littered the bankside. By the look of things, Barry was lucky to be alive. Damn.

Charli looked at Barry. He only shook his head. Part of her was relieved, and part felt guilty for being relieved.

She turned to face the steep hill. "Fred, where did you first see the bear?" Surveying the incline, she realized Fred didn't need to show her. A huge swath of cleared ground led directly up the hill. Looked like a tornado had come down the side. "Never mind, Fred. Got it."

Jed moseyed closer to Charli. "Who's yer friend, Charli?"

She'd been so wrapped up in getting Barry's memory back, she'd forgotten common courtesy. "I'm sorry, Jed. This is my friend Barry. He's . . . uh . . . he's a honey collector." Both men looked at her.

"Right, Barry?" She gave him a face that said *go along with this or I'll kill you later.*

Barry stifled a laugh with a cough. "Yes, honey collector. I examine the honey's texture to see if . . . uh . . . the queen bee is . . . young or old."

Both she and Jed looked at him and said together, "You can do that?"

What the hell? She bonked her head again. That was as true as him being a honey collector. Where in the Sam Hill did *honey collector* come from? She was losing it. Big time.

She started up the slope, using trees to push her forward where the angle was steep. She took a misstep and slid backward. Strong, firm hands wrapped around her waist. Barry let her falling weight bring her closer, her back against his front. Holy fuck, that felt good.

How long had it been since someone had simply held her? Tucked her into a cocoon of warm safety where nothing existed except them? Turning her head to the side, she took in his scent emanating from his unbuttoned collar, the flowing heat his body generated under the jeans and shirt she'd bought him before going into the office this morning. There was no denying it. She wanted this man in her bed, badly.

A rumble vibrated her back. In his eyes, she saw her desire reflected. He wanted her just as much. Butterflies flipped in her stomach.

"Charli, girl. Ya all right over thar?"

She sighed and stepped from Barry's secure grasp. "Yeah, Fred. I'm fine. Just slipped a little."

"Ya needin' help?"

"No help. Thanks, Fred, I got it." The ground flattened, so it was easier to stay upright. They came to a stop in front of a mess of briars and tangled vines.

Fred pointed at it. "I seen the bear hidin' behine this mishmash of vegie-tation." He smiled at Jed standing beside him. "How'd ya like that big word, thar, brother?" Jed congratulated him with a slap on the arm and telling him he was one smart sumbitch.

Charli walked behind the brush pile and couldn't believe her eyes. She hurried back in front and stood between the two men, hooked Fred's arm with one of her own and Jed's with the other. "You guys are the best friends a vet could have." Her steps grew longer. "You take care of your animals, and your mama."

Both boys' cheeks reddened. "Well, Charli," Fred said, "you take good care of us. You know exac'ly where the critter is a hurtin'. It's like ya read their minds or sumpin'. And Ma likes you. Said yer a good *n'flew ants*, or sumpin' like that."

Holding back her laugh, Charli translated. "I'm a good influence. That's nice of your ma to say. I'll have to thank her." They traveled in a single line, traipsing over the steep bottom. Upon reaching the gravel road, Charli once again hooked her arms in one of theirs and headed for their truck.

"You boys have helped us so much here. I don't want to take up any more of your time. I know you got chores awaiting at the farm."

"Yes, ma'am, we do. Say, how's the bear doing after the op-a-rashon?"

"He's doing great." She tilted her head back to yell, "Wouldn't you agree, Barry?"

"Yes, I shor do," he called behind them.

Jed turned to Fred. "He sounds intelligent, don't he?" Fred nodded.

Reaching the Chevy's driver's door, she pecked a kiss on each man's cheek. A sure way to get a shy guy to leave is to show him affection. Both men blushed to the tips of their ears and hurried into the truck. They were so intent on getting away, they didn't even wave.

Barry wrapped his arms around her waist from behind. "What was that all about?"

She leaned into him. "You're going to *sheet yer britches* when I show you." She took his hand, and together they climbed a second time. Upon reaching the brush pile, she dragged him around to the back.

"Holy shit. You're right. What is it?" Both crouched next to a long, half-buried plastic container, the lid crooked. He pulled the top back and a wretched smell of rotten food almost made them gag. Barry reached in and pulled out one of the plastic grocery bags with what looked like spaghetti sauce smeared on it. He pried the knot open to see bundles of hundred-dollar bills. He looked up at Charli, then grabbed another bag. Same contents—except the food clinging to the bag looked fuzzy and green.

"Damn, Barry. There has to be a half million dollars in there. Anything else buried?" Barry rummaged to the far side. His hand brought out a sack containing a beautiful diamond necklace.

"Oh my god, Barry. What were you doing with this? Does any of this look familiar? Is it yours?"

"No." He threw his hands into the air in frustration. "I don't know what this is. I don't know." He stood and walked away. Charli ran after him and grabbed his arm.

"Hey. Look at me." He wouldn't bring his eyes to hers. "Barry, look at me." She laid her palm against his cheek. The pain in his eyes made her want to wrap him up and take away the world. "I know this isn't proceeding as you hoped, but we'll figure it out. It's only noon."

He brought her hand to his lips and kissed each knuckle. "I know. It's just aggravating thinking the answer is around the corner only to find nothing." He rested his forehead against hers.

"We'll find the answers. It just might take a little time. Okay?" God, she really hoped they could get some answers quickly. Fear lodged in her heart for him. She wanted to make sure he was safe and there was nothing for him to be scared of, but without any information, it was hard to know if that was true.

He smiled. "Yeah, okay. What are we going to do with the money? Take it back to the office?"

She debated for a second. In Shedford, nobody trusted corporations. "There's nothing here that warrants us taking it. Maybe it belongs to some old couple who doesn't trust banks, so they buried it. Like keeping their life's saving under the mattress."

That was highly likely. People in her neck of the woods didn't go to the bank. They lived at a different pace and weren't always willing to trust the government or its agencies. She came from a long line of vets, which made it easier for her to get them to trust her. Still, even though she lived in Shedford, she was originally from a big city.

Most of the folks in her town didn't travel anywhere but the main street to go to the shops. Would someone go out so far and bury money and jewelry instead of taking it to a bank and locking it in a safe? Absolutely. Nothing surprised her in that town.

"And that," Barry said, "is why you're the special agent, and I'm the sissy."

She laughed. "Let's cover the box with dirt and brambles, then get some lunch. I'm hungry."

"Sounds good to me."

CHAPTER EIGHT

Klamin watched the woman and bear come down the hill through the scope on his rifle. Wasn't she a nice sight. Pretty face and voluptuous body that would take any beating he could give and come back for more. He'd love for his bear servant to bring her back to the compound. The things he would do with her.

He'd seen her before a couple of times. Never had the chance to really look her over. He was also curious about the rumor he'd heard that said she could talk to animals. A real Doctor Dolittle.

What would his shifters tell her? Would they remember the intense pain of the shock therapy, the continuous blood sharing? Their former selves? That was a chance he wasn't willing to take. He'd worked too hard and too long to let his plans be ruined by one fuckup beyond his control.

Damn hillbillies. He should've shot them when he first saw them on the hillside this morning. He shouldn't have put off clearing the money and jewels until the day before. But he'd been so busy with his new project. It had to be set up carefully with the correct elements or it could prove disastrous, almost like now.

It could be worse. At least they weren't taking the money. Still, he'd have to kill them both. The bear for sure, before he remembered.

What the fuck happened to break his mind control over the shifter? It had to be the amnesia. He'd never lost one before. That wasn't true, but he didn't want to remember those. They were failures. The bear was his shining glory. And it took fucking long enough to get it right.

But after decoding the old recipe, it was as easy as making cereal. His plan would be realized soon and then more wealth and happiness than he'd ever imagined would be his. He liked this area. Might keep his headquarters here in the mountains. They offered the perfect hiding place for the compound, plus he liked the cold weather.

His two targets had reached the road and were heading to the SUV. He aimed the crosshairs on the man rounding the front of the vehicle. He squeezed the trigger.

CHAPTER NINE

With more questions than answers, Barry came down the hill with Charli after hiding the money container. What was his connection to the container? Was it his? Was he really hiding money? And to what purpose? His gut clenched. Maybe someone was after him and trying to rob him.

"What do you want for lunch?" Charli asked.

"Food in general works for me," Barry said as he crossed in front of the SUV. His animal half grabbed control of his body, stopping him in his tracks. Danger floated in the air. A small missile slammed into the truck's side where he would've been had he kept moving. A pop like a firecracker sounded in the trees on the other side of the creek.

"Barry?" Charli had her door open, but leaned back to look over the hood.

He lunged toward the passenger door. "Get in the truck, Charli. Now!" He threw the door open. A hot punch blasted up and down his backside. He growled and fell onto the seat, his hands grabbing the console between them. "Go, Charli, go!"

She glanced at him. "Barry, what—"

"Go!"

She stomped on the gas pedal and the SUV spun its wheels before gripping the ground and darting forward. Charli reached to the side, taking a handful of Barry's shirt, trying to pull him into the seat. "Barry, get your ass in this car now."

He pulled his upper body in far enough for her to grab his belt. A roar rolled out of his throat when she yanked him in. Goddamn, that shit hurt! He tried hard to find his way into the seat but everything was moving too fast.

"Barry, you're bleeding." Her voice was filled with alarm.

"No shit." He pulled a knee onto the floor mat. Another bullet hit the back passenger door. They were in a world of trouble and Barry didn't know why. All he could hope was that he hadn't brought trouble with him. He'd never live with himself knowing his mate was in danger because of him.

"Get in here now!" Charli gripped the steering wheel, afraid to let go, afraid of losing control and rolling over the cliff side.

"Goddammit, woman. I'm trying." Another projectile banged against the truck's backside. Charli swerved, Barry wrestled his other leg onto the floor mat, and the passenger door slammed shut. Kneeling, he lay forward and rested his head on the center console, gritting his teeth.

"Are you shot? Where?" She ran her hand over his back, feeling for wetness on the dark shirt.

"My ass."

Her hand froze. "You're shot in the ass?" What sounded like a snort came from her. "Right or left cheek?"

He roared loudly in pain and humiliation. "What the fuck does it matter? I'm shot."

Biting back a grin, Charli cleared her throat. "Shot in the ass twice in one day. Once as a shifter, once as a human. I think you've set a record for me."

He leaned up, looking at her. "Are you making fun of me? I'm bleeding."

Charli patted him on his head, tempted to glide her fingers through his soft hair. "You are the *butt* of my joke, dear." She barely choked back a laugh.

"Great," he growled. "Am I going to hear ass references for the rest of the day? I could die."

She was so tempted to roll her eyes but decided he might get even more offended if she did. "Don't worry, stud. No one dies from a hole in their ass. You're just fortunate enough to have two ass holes." He groaned and dropped his head onto the console. This time, laughter did erupt from her. Part was from teasing this adorable man, and part a release of absolute terror at the thought of losing him.

A shot in the ass she could fix. Him getting killed was not something her heart wanted to think about. Her jokes were allowing him to focus on himself instead of noticing how tightly she held the steering wheel.

"Why don't you shift? It will heal itself." She took a quick peek at him to ensure he was still hanging on.

"Shifting heals things?" Barry looked dumbfounded. He definitely needed to start with Shifters 101. "How do I shift?"

She glanced at him and gave him a sympathetic look. "You're asking me? Like I have a clue?"

He groaned and dropped his head forward again. "Well, shit. How close are we to a hospital?"

A quick look at the speedometer had her shaking her head. "At least forty-five, fifty minutes. It'll take fifteen to get off this damn mountainside with all the turns."

"I could be dead by then," he grumbled.

She should probably not tell him that a shot to the ass was better than one to the groin.

"As I said, no worries. Your bear is already healing you. We'll be at the clinic in under thirty, and I'll take care of you."

"*Your* clinic, as in *veterinarian*—animals?"

"Chill, bear. Your ass is the same as a horse's. Don't be a jackass about this." She snickered to herself.

He slid a hot hand over her upper thigh, giving a little squeeze. She gasped at the tingles running straight to her core. His fingers spread, heating more than just her leg. She tried to move his hand away, but he only gripped her tighter.

Fuck, he was killing her, making her wet and wanting. A low growl reached her ears. "Hey, don't blame me this time. Would you like me to spank your ass to get your mind off me?"

"You can spank me any time you want, darlin'. After you take the bullet out. But breathing you in, thinking of your taste, overpowers all the pain."

Aw, damn. She bit her lip to keep from melting in her seat. "So, you're saying I'm like morphine?"

"You are a powerful drug, baby, and I'm completely addicted."

She rolled her eyes. "For having no memory, you remember the cheesiest come-ons. If you say you want to be my socks to stay with me every step of the way, I'll kick your ass *before* I take out the bullet. Whoever came up with that line is a complete moron. *Single* moron, at that."

Barry barked out a laugh. "That's quite original. I think. I'll never use it, but it's different."

Charli slowed the SUV and turned onto the highway running past her rock driveway. Good, she'd gotten his mind off the smoking hole in his butt. Now all she needed was to get him fixed up. "We're almost there. Sit tight. Oh wait, you can't sit." She slapped the steering wheel with a giggle.

Barry rubbed his face with his hands and groaned. "Will I ever hear the end of this?"

Charli smiled. "Not if I have my way."

An hour later, Barry lay ass-end up on the steel operating table in the animal clinic. The bleeding had stopped, the bear healing it over. Charli needed to recut the top of the hole to get inside.

"This shouldn't hurt much. I gave you a local anesthetic, and the bear has done a good job of healing from the bottom up." And what a great bottom lay before her. Tight, with the perfect amount of bubble for her to squeeze to her heart's desire. Not that she should be thinking of that during something so serious, but damn, the guy had the glutes of a god.

She rubbed a gloved hand over the globes. She would've loved skin to skin, but she was done up in scrubs and surgical attire and wasn't willing to risk infection. That would mean more chances to see and handle the merchandise, though. Until that moment, she hadn't realized she had this kind of love for a sexy ass.

Barry took a deep breath. "Dammit, woman. You're doing it again. You smell so good, and I'm stuck facedown. It's hard for a man to lie on his stomach when he's hard."

She bit the inside of her cheek to keep from laughing at his dilemma. It sucked for him because she had a great, oh so great, view of his backside. She gently patted his uninjured ass cheek. "I hardly noticed your hardness. Now be quiet while I dig this out. It shouldn't be that hard."

"That's what you think." He grunted and laid his head on his hands.

Never before had Charli talked this easily with someone. The one-liners came with little effort, Barry bringing out the fun in her. A part she hadn't seen since school. She could get used to having someone around. "Someone"—or only him?

CHAPTER TEN

With sandwich and chips on a plate and a glass of water with a straw, Charli walked into her living room. One of the best asses she'd ever handled—and she did handle this one as much as she could—lay on the sofa waiting for lunch.

She smiled seeing his gorgeous eyes. "Hey, *butt*ercup, how's it going?"

Barry groaned. "How many more ass and butt jokes do you have?"

"Hey"—she set the food and drink on the coffee table—"don't be a shithead. If you still hurt, I'll bring you some *ass*pirin."

He looked up at her from his position lying on his stomach. "Really?"

"Oh, *butt* wait. I'd like to thank you for busting your ass out there. I knew you had one smart ass . . . or are you just a wise ass?"

"No! Stop!" Barry guffawed. "I can't stand being the butt of your jokes. Nor can I stand."

Charli plopped down on a swivel chair. "Whew, I'm glad that's over."

"Really? You're done now?" he gave her a skeptical look.

She nodded. "Yeah. I'm pooped."

A grin broke over his lips and his laughter thundered in the house.

She leaped from her chair, headed for the kitchen. Barry reached out and snagged her leg. "Get your ass over here, woman." Trying to pull out of his grasp, laughing turned to snorting, and she slipped to the floor. From his prone position on the sofa, his arm slid her across the hardwood to where he lay. The guy had serious muscles to be able to do that with her curvy body.

He chuckled like a pirate. "Now you're mine, wench." His hand wrapped around the back of her head and pulled her close, bringing her lips to his.

The kiss was all-consuming. He took her mouth hard, with a wildness that left her breathless. Almost as if she'd just run a marathon. The spikes of adrenaline inside her sent fire to her core. There was no doubt where this was going. She'd wanted him from the moment their eyes met and now it was their time. He growled softly by her lips, his tongue dancing over hers and sucking it into his mouth.

Her body took over. The feel of his hands gliding down to slip under her shirt only urged her on. With nimble fingers, he removed her top and drew circles with his tongue over her collarbone. Her respiration faltered. She'd never had a man touch her to the point that her insides melted. He skimmed his mouth over her cute lacy bra. Thank god she'd worn the nice one today. Too bad the top didn't match the bottom, but she doubted he'd care.

He kissed his way down to her belly button, bit the small indentation, and then twirled his tongue in circles over it. Lust clawed at her chest. Her body throbbed with her need for release.

Her legs shook like she'd been working out for hours. Anticipation made her almost giddy as he continued to kiss his way down to her hips. She gulped unsteady breaths. He hooked his hands in her pants and dragged them down her legs. Then it came time for her underwear. For a second, common sense tried to hit her in the head, but desire slammed the door closed on it.

Muscles strung tightly, she watched as he tugged her tiny bikini underwear down. She didn't care if she was a bigger girl, she still wore the stuff she felt sexy in. That was part of who she was. Her heartbeat pounded in her head. She breathed so fast, she swore she'd pass out. His gaze lifted from between her legs to meet hers. Oh damn. That look of pure ownership he gave her made her channel slicker.

Then he did it. Oh, he went straight for the kill. He licked her pussy in a slow, drawn-out caress. Lord have mercy!

"I can't fucking wait any longer," he growled.

Stars exploded behind her lids. She moaned out a curse and begged as she drew breath. Fire spread in her veins. This was new, amazing, and totally different from any man. Desperation bloomed inside her. Barry was so good with his tongue. Too good. He rumbled a soft sweet word and she saw heaven. Even in the middle of this, he still managed to call her beautiful.

"Barry . . ."

He stopped, and she bit back a curse. What the hell was wrong with him? Why would he stop *now*?

"Listen to me carefully, sweetheart," he said, and she could hear the roughness of his bear in his voice. "I'm going to eat your sweet pussy like no fucking man has ever done before. My mouth, my tongue, and my teeth are going to own you. With every lick and suck, I'm going to take you and stamp your scent on my face. All mine."

She gulped at the proprietary note in his voice. He licked up her pussy lips and she groaned at the way her channel grasped at nothing. "Every drop of your honey belongs to me." He licked a circle around her clit. "Every moan. Every groan. Everything. And when you come"—he fondled her with his tongue for a millisecond and she almost cried— "and you will come like the world is fucking ending, you're going to know that I'm the only fucking man you want in your body. Me. Only me. No other. Only I have the right to be here."

He slid a finger into her pussy. Her channel contracted around his digit in a tight grip. "That's right, baby. When the time comes, it's going to be my dick in you. My cock pounding your pussy and making you mine. My name being screamed from your gorgeous lips."

He thrust his tongue into her and growled. The vibration made her entire body shudder. Whimpers slipped past her lips at the same moment that shakes rattled her core. She wiggled her sex closer to his face. Another lick. Up to her tight little nubbin and down to her ass. Repeat. He knew just how to touch her, how to make her melt.

Lust roared louder inside her, almost as if she were the shifter. Animalistic desire had her panting and tense, ready for her body to burst into flames. Arousal gathered hot and tight at the very spot he continued to lick mercilessly. She was close, so close. Her body screamed for her to hurry and give in or she'd die a slow death. Heat skyrocketed inside her. Perspiration coated her skin. More. Faster. She needed him to get her there, over the edge.

"Barry, I need . . ."

Him. Now. Preferably moving at a faster pace.

The feel of his teeth and tongue circling and nibbling her bundled flesh was more than she could take. Electric currents zoomed through her and pushed her off that final ledge. He growled again. The vibration increased her pleasure. High. Higher. So high she swore and shook with the force of her release. Her body jerked under his lips. He continued to lick her, sucking, rubbing his face on her wet folds.

Holy mother of vibrators. The bear had a tongue that needed insuring. Breaths came in short, ragged puffs. Fuck breathing, she could die at that moment and it would have all been worth it. All the years without sex and her inability to find a man who could touch her in the ways she desired. They'd disappeared with a single lick of Barry's tongue on her girl parts. Barry pushed back. His face had turned into a feral mask of desire. Wild hunger had taken over his features. His nostrils flared, his jaw clenched, and the vein on the side of his neck throbbed. Fuck. Looking at him made her pussy quiver—again.

"What's wrong?" she asked hoarsely.

He inhaled and groaned. "You smell so fucking good. I can't— Your taste? Delicious. It's hard for me to control this bear. The animal side is aggressive. He wants you. All he keeps demanding is to take you. To fuck you until all you have is my seed deep in your body, marking you as mine." His gaze clashed with hers. "To fuck you. To watch my cum drip out of your slit. He wants me to make you mine again and again, until your legs can't hold you up and they're shaking from how hard you come."

Goddamn that was sexy. Oh so sexy. She could see the way he struggled to control his animal. "Barry, I love how much you want me right now. Hell, I feel like I'm in curvy girl heaven, but I think you need a little time getting to know your bear before we—you know."

He licked his lips. Oh dear god, he licked his lips and the golden light in his eyes grew brighter. A short rumble later and he nodded. "You're right. I need to learn control before we go further." He crawled up her body and pressed his hard erection into the juncture of her thighs. His lips brushed over hers. The taste of her own body made her slick all over again. "I'm going to have you soon. Very soon."

God, she hoped so.

CHAPTER ELEVEN

Devin leaned over his desk, the two case files neatly aligned, showing shots from both the bank and jewelry store robberies. No signs of forced entry at either location. No prints at any door or window. Unless the perp was a ghost who could walk through walls, he was stumped at the moment.

"Wassup, Sonder?" Russel shuffled up to his desk.

"Looking over the files Detective Gibbons brought this morning."

"Man, is she hot or what. I'd sniff a mile to see where she pees."

Devin turned to his coworker, face dead serious. "Is that because you're a horny toad?" Russel stared at his eyes, probably trying to figure out if he was serious or not. Devin had a dry sense of humor and he loved to screw with other people's heads. He decided to let Russel off the hook. "I'm joking, Mayer." Devin slapped Russel's back.

Russel's tense body relaxed. "Right." He smiled. "Gotcha, there."

Devin turned back to the pictures and various papers. "Nothing looks out of the ordinary for the human world. If it is a shifter committing these crimes, then, I don't know. Maybe they have magic."

"Nah, dude. Magic isn't real. It's aliens." Devin raised a brow at him. "Yeah, seriously. Those little fuckers are slippery. Mean as hell, too."

"You've personally met an alien?"

"Not really. But my sister's boyfriend's cousin swears he did. They were hiking somewhere out east and said they saw a ship rise out of the ground. Well, not really a ship, but something like a ship. Then guards with dogs chased them away. And when they went back the next day, the mountain was gone."

"A mountain? Gone?"

Russel shrugged. "That's what they said. Personally, I think they were high, but what do I know?"

"Well"—Devin wiped a hand over his brow—"let's eliminate aliens, for right now. Sound good?"

"Yup, works for me. I'm just saying."

"No, I get it. Keep an open mind, right? We're dealing with more than human stuff," Devin said.

"Right, right." Russel rubbed his hands together. "So did the footage of the naked—I mean, the video come in for either burglary?"

Devin sat in his chair and wiggled the mouse on its pad. "Just got it from the detective. Haven't looked through it yet." Russel leaned over Devin so closely, Devin could feel his body heat. "Uh, Mayer, would you like to join in?"

Mayer slapped him on the back hard enough to shove his chair forward, mashing him against the desk. "Yeah, sure, man. Thanks for asking." He rolled in a seat from the empty desk on the other side of the partition. "Okay, whatcha got?"

Devin clicked the Play button on the computer monitor. A grayscale image of a small, narrow room popped onto the screen. On the back wall looked to be a door with a keypad next to it. The time code at the bottom of the screen read 03:34, between three and four in the morning.

At the top of the screen, the door from the outer hall opened and the figure of a woman with thick black hair to her waist walked in.

Half the hair was combed forward, covering her face. Only the tip of her nose showed. Now Devin understood why they couldn't ID the woman by sight.

She stopped at the keypad, and with a long, sharp fingernail she pushed the buttons, and the door popped open. And that would be why there were no strange fingerprints at the crime scenes. No, she couldn't do everything with only nails. There had to be a print somewhere.

The shot on the screen changed to inside the vault. The woman quickly loaded stacks of money into plastic bags hanging on her arm. When the bags were full, she left both rooms. Since the hall was part of the employee-only area, with only the break room across the hall, there were no cameras monitoring it. Just the vault rooms. That was probably changing now.

Devin clicked the Stop button on the video. "Well, that was sort of strange."

Russel snorted. "Couldn't even see anything." Devin was sure Russel wasn't referring to the thief's face.

"Let's see what else is included." He clicked the green triangle on the screen and the image changed to a long hallway with several offices to the sides. The big door at the far end had a sign: Banking Personnel Only. "That must be the hall leading to the bank lobby." The time at the bottom of the screen coincided with the other angles. "So there should be a person walking through the shot to get out of the building."

After several seconds of nothing, Devin fast-forwarded the image. A streak of something dark flashed and had him rewinding a bit. He hit Play to watch a fluffy black cat slowly strolling into one of the offices.

Russel recoiled in his chair. "Eww. I hate cats."

"What's wrong with cats?" Devin turned his poker face to Russel.

"They give me the willies. Those fuckers are worse than aliens. Especially with their sharp-ass claws."

"You mean like this?" Devin lifted a hand and morphed it into his panther's paw, claws extended.

Russel scrambled his chair back, hand over his heart. "Don't do that, man. You scared the shit out of me. I'll have nightmares for a month now."

Devin laughed. "You can't be serious."

"Oh, I'm as serious as the heart attack you just about gave me. Shit."

Director Milkan stuck his head over the wall partition. "What are y'all doing? Sinatra, you screaming like a girl again?"

"It wasn't my fault this time." He pointed to Devin, then looked at Milkan. "When did you get in?"

"Just walked in to hear your lovely singing." Milkan looked at the computer monitor. "Are those the security shots from the bank?"

Devin pivoted his chair toward the other two. "They are. I can see why the police are stumped. Doesn't show much but a woman with long hair disappearing after robbing the vault."

"What about the jewelry store?" Milkan asked.

"Haven't received that footage yet. I think we need to check out both places for ourselves," Devin said. "Get a feel for everything."

"It's been weeks since the robberies." Milkan shrugged. "Probably won't be anything to find that's not contaminated in some way."

"Maybe." Devin stood and pulled on his suit jacket.

"All right," Milkan said, stepping back. "I'll buy us lunch on the way. Let's go."

CHAPTER TWELVE

Devin pushed open a door from the sidewalk with the name Stevens Jewelry etched into the glass. Overhead, a brass bell rattled. A tall saleswoman approached from the side.

"Mr. Milkan. It's lovely to see you again." She reached out to shake Milkan's hand. His cheeks flushed a light pink.

"Uh, yes. Good to see you, too."

"How does your wife like the earrings you bought her?"

"She loves them. You were right about the cut. Should never question a lady who knows her jewelry." The woman laughed. After an awkward second, Milkan continued. "We're here to see Mr. Stevens." He pulled a business card from his inside pocket and handed it to her.

She glanced at it. "I didn't know you were with the police. Special unit?"

Russel leaned forward. "Yeah, we investigate the freaky shit." Both men discreetly backhanded him. "What? We do," he whispered liked a scorned little kid. The lady disappeared into a back room. A minute later a short, balding man hurried from the back, hand extended.

"Director Milkan. Thank you for coming. Do you have any news on my stolen merchandise?"

"No, sir, we don't. But we'd like to have another look around, if we could."

The man looked dejected. "S-sure, I don't think there is anything here that will help. The glass with the hole cut into it was replaced last week. The other police took it with them." He pointed to a cabinet displaying a ton of bling. Devin thought one piece of that crap would cost his entire year's salary. He didn't understand why women had to have it so badly. If he ever met a woman, he wouldn't be buying anything so useless. He'd consider power tools, though.

Devin whispered to Milkan, "Why was there a hole cut in the glass?"

"Because the cabinets are hooked up to alarms. If they slide open or if the glass is smashed through, then alarms immediately sound."

"Ah, so the thief had done her homework. Could it be an inside job?"

The director paused. "I wonder if the PD thought of that. I'd like to get the cutter back. Let's get a look at the employees for long black hair." He called to the owner. "Mr. Stevens, do you mind if we walk in the employee areas?"

Stevens stood behind one of the counters. They could barely see the top of his head. "Please do. Everything is through the door there." The men headed around the counter and followed the aisle through the single door marked Employees Only.

The back rooms were much less spacious than the showroom. Seemed they had an open door policy, which helped. They could walk by and peek in without making a big fuss. A man and a woman with short sandy hair shared an office that had Accounting on the door. Scratch her off the list of candidates.

The next office belonged to the office manager. She sat at her desk, working on her computer. A pile of papers was neatly stacked and arranged by color on a table. On the floor in front of shelves lay a bunched-up old blanket flattened in the middle, possibly for a small child or animal to sleep on. Binders on the shelves were arranged by color, ring width, and height. A printed label graced each spine perfectly.

This could be the woman of his dreams. Devin stepped up to introduce himself, felt a bump on his hip, and the next thing he knew, he was staring at the ceiling, flat on his back. The manager flew from her desk and was at his side in a second.

"Oh my. Are you all right?" she asked. Her dark hair shone under the fluorescent lights, a long braid slid over her shoulder. Her face had the clearest complexion with straight pearly-white teeth. Perfection.

Another lady in an apron with a company logo consisting of a mop and bucket put her hand under his back and helped him sit up. "I am so sorry, sir. I didn't see you standing there." She straightened her apron and the handkerchief covering a bun at the bottom of her head. The cleaning woman didn't look to have the strength to knock him to the ground, but she clearly had.

Devin shook his head to clear the spinning. "I'm sorry. It was my fault for not watching where I was going." Both ladies helped him to his feet. The cleaning lady slipped off her rubber gloves and wiped down the back of his black jacket while he faced a very lovely lady. He glanced at her soft hands on his arm and saw a wedding ring. Of course. He should've known better.

"There you go, sir," the cleaning lady said. "Back to where you were."

He stepped away. "Thank you, ladies, for your assistance. I need to catch up with the others. Have a good day." He hurried away before he made more of a fool of himself.

The other two men stepped out of the small break room. Smelled like someone had heated up spaghetti in the microwave. Good thing they'd eaten lunch already, or he might search out that container.

Russel sniffed loudly and turned to face him. "Devin, my man, where have you been? I smell pussy all over you. And I'm not talking the juicy kind that's good to eat."

Immediately Devin's thoughts turned to the pretty office manager and how he'd embarrassed himself by falling into her office. He tried to keep his emotions neutral so the other shifter wouldn't smell his shame.

"Sinatra, we need to get you your woman so she can stick something in your mouth to keep you quiet."

Russel laughed and slapped him on the arm. "Now you're talking!"

Devin glimpsed a door next to the break room. An alarm keypad was attached to the wall beside the door frame. "Did you go through there?"

Russel shook his head as Devin opened the door. Cool fresh air zipped past him from outside. Several cars sat in a small asphalted area between the back of this building and the next. A dumpster sat next to a small access lane. Normal employee parking lot.

Milkan looked back at them from the other end of the hall. "Y'all done playing around?" He glanced down at his watch. "It's time to leave. Isn't anything here."

The group entered the showroom and waved to the saleswoman on their way out the door. As they stepped onto the front sidewalk, police cruisers raced down Main, sirens blaring, headed out of town.

Russel licked his lips. "Speaking of pussy, I wonder if the delicious Detective Gibbons is available."

Milkan laughed. "Sinatra, that woman will put you on your ass before you get close enough to hit on her."

Russel smiled. "That's what I'm hoping for."

Devin shook his head and smiled.

CHAPTER THIRTEEN

Charli woke from her nap aching for her and Barry to go the extra step. As it was, her body was pissed as hell she had to spend time with her vibrator while Barry had gone out for a quick walk to take the edge off. Still, she'd woken up happier than she'd ever been. Could Barry really be her mate? When she was told about shifters after joining the fellowship, she had a million questions that were never really answered. She needed Shifters 101 as badly as Barry did.

She reached her hand out to the other side of the bed, wanting to feel hot, taut skin, but found only cold sheet. "Barry?" She sat up and looked around the room. Hearing no reply, she donned a robe and headed to the kitchen. Maybe he was raiding her fridge. She'd yet to meet a shifter who didn't seem to be constantly hungry.

No one in the kitchen or living room. Maybe he was in the barn? After quickly throwing on clothes, Charli hurried to the clinic. The lights were off and the door was locked as usual. She went around the side of the building to the stalls. Still no sign of him. "Barry!"

A hundred horrible thoughts ran through her mind. Had his memory come back and he left? She'd never see him again. Had his mind snapped and he turned into his animal and ran off as a new wildlife addition to the forest?

She wandered to the horse corral behind the barn, pain tearing at her heart. What the fuck was she thinking falling for a complete stranger? But the animal called her *mate*. Could shifter animals lie? Why the fuck not? Everyone else sure did. Men had lied to her so much in the past that she never knew what to believe. It was a wonder she trusted anyone at all, but she knew not everyone was the same. That didn't mean she couldn't be lied to again. But why?

On the worn dirt path leading into the horse enclosure, bear prints tracked around the side toward the trees. The paw impressions had to be his. She followed the trail to the woods, where she lost sight of his direction. Fortunately, this side of the mountain led to the main road into town and the turn-off where Fred and Jed had found Barry.

That was all the evidence she needed to head back to the hillside next to the creek and rockslide. Her panicked mind knew of nothing else to grab on to.

Hauling ass along the twisting, turning highway, she came around a curve and slammed on her brakes. The roadside was lined with police cars and flashing lights and men in uniform milling around, looking over the side of the road.

The metal guardrail was torn away, and she noted rappelling ropes were fastened around thick trees. Looked like a vehicle had run off the road and rolled down the steep incline to the creek. She didn't rubber-neck since she was on a mission to find Barry.

After another mile, Charli slowed for the turn onto the gravel road heading up the mountain. She took a deep breath and told herself everything was going to be fine. She needed to keep a positive attitude, stop thinking only the worst. Fuck, all she could think was every possible scenario that ended up with Barry being in a morgue. She needed to dial the drama back in her mind and just focus on what she could do.

Carefully, yet quickly, she drove the narrow lane, watching for clues of Barry's passing—human or animal. Through the thick tree trunks lining the ground between the road and creek, Charli thought she saw a boat on the water. The creek was high this time of year from the autumn rain showers. Powering a johnboat would be easy, and several locals fished about every day.

She slowed the SUV, waiting for the boat to pass an opening in the tree line. Holy shit. She couldn't see the man's face, but he was as naked as naked could get. Seeing that's how she met Barry, she'd bet the farm and wiener dog that was him.

Honking the horn, she tried to get his attention. Either he didn't hear it or he just didn't acknowledge it. One eye on the road and one on the creek, she approached the turn just before the rockslide. Again Charli slowed, hoping the boat would stop, but it puttered past. Damn.

The next turn took her farther from the creek than she wanted. Driving faster than she should, Charli dodged potholes and small boulders. She maneuvered a hairpin curve, then descended the hill to flat terrain. Off in the distance, a white fence wrapped around a grassy field with a copse of mangled-looking trees in the center. Being in the middle of nowhere, she couldn't imagine anyone living out here.

With a lot more patience than she felt she had, she brought the SUV to a stop before an old bridge crossing the creek. She waited, hoping Barry hadn't passed by or stopped somewhere upstream. Too nervous to sit in the truck, Charli hopped out and shuffled closer to the water. Her hands felt like icicles from how tensed she'd been while driving. Relaxing her body and mind, she listened for the sound of a motor in the quiet of nature.

Instead of the whine of an engine, she heard grunts and scuffles coming from . . . below the bridge. Edging by the concrete alongside the road, she made her way down the bankside enough to peer underneath the bridge.

Oh fuck. It was Barry. Naked and taking huge, stuffed orange bags from the boat and shoving them onto a concrete shelf under the iron girder.

"Barry! What are you doing?" Charli slid down the remaining bankside and approached a zombielike Barry. She pulled on his arm, trying to get his attention. "Barry?" Again she yanked on him when he turned toward the boat sitting on the side. "What are—"

To her surprise, he whipped around and wrapped his hands around her throat. His squeeze was so tight she couldn't even gasp in a breath. Charli looked into his eyes; his focus was off in the distance.

Barry?

Nothing. Her pulse kicked up at the base of her throat. *Barry!* The empty look remained, and his mechanical movements didn't help the situation.

Barry, answer me. I need you. Silence. She couldn't connect with the animal inside him. This wasn't her Barry. Fuck!

Feeling her windpipe move, she realized the lights were on, but no one was home, not even the bear. In this state, it was clear he had no idea what he was doing. She had to take immediate action or risk him killing her. Her knee smashed into his groin. As he bent in half, his hold loosened, but didn't release. Charli slammed her fists onto his elbows, ripping his fingers from her. Then she smashed his temple with the back of her elbow. With Barry off balance, she shoved him into the frigid water.

Popping up through the water, head thrown back, Barry sputtered and stumbled on the creek-bed rocks.

"What the fuck?" He looked around, confusion on his face. "Charli, where are we? Why am I naked in this freezing water?" He muscled his way to shore. She rubbed a hand over her throat and watched him cautiously. This was the Barry she knew.

Charli took off her coat and wrapped it around his shoulders; it didn't cover the huge man much, but it was all she could do. "Barry," she took his face in her hands, focusing his attention on her. "What were you doing?"

He looked at the boat and bridge. "I don't know. Last thing I remember was lying in bed with you. How did I get here? Where is here?"

Her heart tripped in her chest. He looked so lost, almost like he was afraid to figure things out. "We're not far from the rockslide where Fred and Jed found you. You don't remember anything? What's in the bags?"

He looked over his shoulder at the orange sacks. "I don't know." He made his way under the bridge. Scratches marred his arms and legs as if he'd walked through a brush pile. The cool ground probably soothed the cuts on his feet. She needed to remember to lather on the disinfectant when they got back.

He opened the large bag and pulled out one of many sacks the size of a bowling ball. Taking off the tie, the top revealed stacks of twenty-dollar bills. Shit just got real. "Oh my god. Do all the bags have money?" Barry searched the other bags and nodded. "How many of the orange bags are there?"

What the hell was going on? Was Barry a millionaire trying to hide his money? How did he not remember any of that? He moved the sacks on the concrete shelf. "I think there are six, including the one in the boat. That could be a quarter million dollars."

"Where did it come from?" Charli asked. Her gut twisted in knots. Instinct told her there was something not right going on.

Barry shivered when a crisp breeze blew under the bridge. "I don't know. And I don't know why I have it. What should we do?"

Charli sighed. For all she knew, it could be his money. Then again, it really could belong to someone else. With so many small business owners in Shedford shoving money in the unlikeliest of places, she really wasn't surprised they found that there.

One time, she'd found a box filled with hundreds of dollars at a farm she'd gone to, to handle a horse giving birth. Another time, she'd been helping a cow lying under a tree in a field when she was hit in the back of the head by a bag that had fallen from the tree. The bag had been stuffed with priceless coins and jewelry the owners thought would be safe in the tree branches.

This finding money? That wasn't really new. And she knew if it didn't belong to Barry, someone living nearby would probably know it was there. One thing folks did not do in Shedford was steal from each other or take something that was likely someone else's.

She glanced at the sun lowering on the horizon. They were running out of time.

Barry broke through her thoughts. "It's getting late. We're going to start losing light quickly. Should we take the money with us?"

"I can't think of a safer place than here, wherever here is. The only people who know it's here are you and me. If it belongs to one of the locals, they're probably going to check on their loot soon. If it belongs to you, well, you know where it's at. Until we find out for sure, it would be very suspicious if someone found it in the SUV."

Decision made, they climbed the creek side toward the truck. Charli noted the bullet wound on his sexy butt cheek was totally gone.

A set of red marks from her nails dragging over his ass would be a good addition. It was time to work on that. Anything to keep from thinking what this was all about. She didn't have a good feeling. She had him back, and that was all that mattered at the moment.

Barry sucked in a deep breath. "I like whatever you're thinking, baby."

CHAPTER FOURTEEN

Charli laughed at the loud huff coming from Barry.

"Ow, woman. What the hell are you thinking?" Barry yanked his foot away from Charli's hold. He lay on the steel surgical table for the second time that day.

"For a big bad bear, you are the biggest baby." She set the cotton ball on the table next to the antibacterial ointment. "At least you can heal with the gashes cleaned out."

Barry swung his legs over the side of the examination table and sat up. "Oh yeah. I forgot that being a shifter heals me faster. Any other jewels of knowledge you'd like to share?"

"Yes. I'm hungry. Let's go back to the house."

Barry closed the white lab jacket he wore once again and pulled the door shut behind them. "You've got a great place here. Mountains, lakes, peace and quiet." He gently took her hand in his.

"I love it here. I don't think I can live anywhere else. Plus, I'm the only vet for the farmers and larger animals in a hundred miles." She opened the door to the kitchen and felt Barry *very* close behind her.

Charli raised a brow. "Before you get any ideas, mister, I want food I can chew and swallow."

A sly grin graced his face. "I got your swallow right here."

Charli rolled her eyes and flipped on the small TV, then headed for the fridge to see what looked good. "How about leftover pot roast and potatoes?" She pulled out a plastic bowl covered with a snap-on lid.

"That'll work. Any steaks?"

She set the bowl on the small island and opened the freezer. After digging around, two T-bones sat next to the bowl.

"Since they're frozen, we'll have to eat them tomorrow. Maybe you can grill. Weather's supposed to be nice." She glanced at the TV, seeing if the weather was on. Instead, "Breaking News" flashed on the screen. "Barry, turn up the volume, will you?"

The face of one of the local reporters filled the screen. "Police aren't sure why the armored truck skidded across the lane, but the path it rolled to the ravine is very evident." Cutaway shots of the upside-down vehicle and investigators walking the area next to the creek flashed by. "The truck was on its regular route to Shedford to drop off money and paychecks for tomorrow's payday. Being Friday and the middle of the month, the truck was carrying twice the amount it normally carried."

The anchor at the news station asked, "Any injuries reported?"

"The driver and front passenger were taken to the hospital and are expected to be fine. But the guard in the back of the truck was found deceased with a slash wound on his neck. The medical examiner will determine the cause of death after an autopsy."

"Do the police have any idea what happened to the stolen orange money bags?" the anchor asked.

"They say the investigation is just starting and more information will be announced later." The reporter signed off.

Barry turned down the volume. Charli stared at him. He wouldn't meet her eyes. Did he think he was the one who killed the guard and took the money? She had to admit the evidence was quite damning. She knew, though, in her heart and without a doubt, that he couldn't have committed those crimes. Her Barry wasn't a bad guy.

Really? What about when he tried to choke you to death?

Okay, maybe there was something else wrong with him. It was like he'd been sleepwalking or zombified. Great. All she needed was to start thinking of Barry as a zombie. Those kinds of romances never ended well. Still, she was sure that in his conscious mind he wasn't going to hurt her.

Without a word, Barry walked out the sliding glass door onto the back porch. Charli's heart skipped. Was he leaving her? She hurried around the island toward the door. In the night air, he leaned against the railing, head down.

"Barry, you don't know if you were part of that robbery or not." She tried to keep her voice nonaccusatory because she didn't want to make him feel worse.

He didn't move to look at her. "Come on, Charli. Even I can't deny the connection: The boat, orange money bags, the timing. My god, Charli. I killed someone and can't remember a damn thing about it."

She wrapped her arms around him from behind, and he turned to hold her in his arms. He laid his cheek on her head and took a deep breath. She didn't know what to say. She didn't want to put Barry in danger, but the risk of not looping in Director Milkan was greater than staying silent. Milkan would know what to do.

"Barry, we've got to go see Milkan again first thing in the morning."

The only sign of his agreement was a nod of his head on her hair. She pulled away and whipped out her cell phone from her back pocket. "Better yet, we can call him right now."

Barry laid his hand on the phone. "Charli, wait." She met his eyes with a questioning look. "How well do you know your boss? Are you sure he won't just throw me in jail? What if the police find out I'm a shifter? The government would take me and experiment and run tests until I have no blood left. What if they outright kill me? I'm not ready to die yet."

Her breathing hitched. Him being gone from her life forever brought an ache to her heart. She was glad the night hid her emotions. It was too soon to have the feelings she did about this man. She stepped back into his arms. It was cold without him.

"Okay, Barry. But I'm calling first thing in the morning. Maybe sleeping on it is for the best—besides, it's late and I'm tired."

"And hungry, if I remember correctly, which I do, for once."

Charli leaned back and smiled up at him. He lowered his lips to hers, taking his time tasting and relishing. Breathless, he released her sweetness. "Charli, I'm not ready to let you go yet. I can't give you up after holding you for only a few hours. Please. Give us time to figure out this craziness."

She agreed. She wasn't ready to give him up either. There had to be a logical explanation that answered all the questions and kept him innocent. Please, God, let there be a happy ending.

Barry held her away from him. "Charli, I'm afraid I'll wander off again or hurt you. I couldn't live with myself if I did. I want you to lock me in one of the clinic's cages tonight."

"What? Lock you in? But that's—" No! That was wrong. A lump formed in her throat at the idea of having Barry in a cage, any cage.

"That's the best and safest thing to do." Another sly grin graced his face. "Plus, who knows, maybe I like being tied up like the wild beast I am."

CHAPTER FIFTEEN

Well, shit. Charli rolled to the other side of the bed and buried her face in the pillow he'd slept on. She couldn't get enough of his smell, his taste.

After taking blankets and pillows from the guest room to the cage in the clinic, she'd watched him lie down, then locked the chain-link door before saying goodnight.

This was so stupid. She was an adult. Why was she denying herself something that felt as needed as water and air? She threw off the covers, let her gown slip from her shoulders, and donned a robe. She slid open her toy drawer and pulled out lube, cuffs, and her golden vibe.

If she stopped to think about what she was doing, she'd probably change her mind, but this was her moment to be the woman she knew lived inside her. Sexually open. Barry had given her too many sexual thoughts. It was time to ease her lust and get her hands on him. All over him. With all her stuff in her robe's pockets, she headed to the clinic. Screw waiting. Her need for him had grown with every second they spent together.

Inside the clinic, her eyes adjusted to the low light of the single lamp on one of the desks she sometimes worked at. Barry lay on his back on the blankets she'd set up in the cage. His chest rose and fell with every breath he took.

"Charli . . ."

Her pussy ached at the low, rough way he said her name, full of need and wanting. She swiped her tongue over her lower lip. Oh boy. The keys shook in her hand. Stupid lust making her all jelly-legged. She should say something. Anything. Instead, she opened the cage and slipped inside, locking it behind her. The keys went back into her very full robe pocket.

"Charli," he mumbled again, his voice rough.

He sat up, his eyes bright with his bear. There was an obvious animalistic quality to his features. His eyes pierced her to what felt like her very soul. He lifted his head, inhaling deeply. Then he licked his lips and she thought she might melt then and there.

Sure, she could have stopped to think about the fact that she hardly knew him or that he could be a dangerous criminal with no memory of his crimes, but she didn't. At that moment, all she knew was that his eyes held her captive. His lips curved into that *I'm gonna fuck you brain-dead* smile, and her hormones ignored all common sense. Screw everything but the here and now. She wanted him and she'd be damned if she wouldn't have him.

She undid her robe and lowered to straddle his legs. His arms tensed as he gripped the sides of the blankets. He didn't give her a chance to say anything. Lips met and fire erupted from the depths of her core. Clothes came off in a rush. It was like they'd hit fast-forward on the remote control of life and neither wanted to wait a second longer. She'd wasted enough time trying not to let her emotions control her, but it was too late. She hadn't been in control from the moment she'd laid eyes on his gorgeous body.

Before she knew what was going on, she was on her back—completely naked—with Barry gazing at her body like she was a work of art. A beautiful masterpiece. Her robe and his clothes lay in a pile next to the blankets, within easy reach, and she remembered the stuff she'd brought with her. She pulled the robe toward her and brought out the toy, cuffs, and lube.

Barry's eyes brightened further, and she loved watching the muscles of his belly clench with his ragged breathing.

"What is this?"

She smiled, her heart filled with an emotion she refused to identify, and winked at him. "I'm sure you can figure out how to use them."

His brows rose and gave him the look of a curious little boy. Damn this man and all his expressions. Every look, every grinding of his jaw or flaring of his nose turned her into a mass of need. "Charli, I don't know—"

She shook her head and lifted her hands to the cage bars, curling her fingers around the cool metal, all the while watching him. "*I* know. I trust you. The keys are in my robe pocket." She bit her lip and glanced down his body. Oh, the man had muscles on him and a sprinkle of hair on his chest that did things to her she'd never imagined hair would do. "Go ahead and put them on me." She winked at him. "It'll be fun."

The sound of the cuffs clicking closed and rough breathing filled the space. He sat back, once again taking in her naked body, and raised a hand to caress her face. He slid his fingers lightly down her jaw to her chest and traced a circle over her nipple. The aching point hardened with his touch. He brought his head closer, his gaze stuck on hers. He looked like he couldn't get enough. She'd never felt so desired in her life.

He struck fast, latching onto a nipple, and sucked. Good lord, that felt unbelievable. She couldn't hold in the loud moan that escaped her throat. Her hips did an involuntary jerk into his hardness. Her channel slickened. He grunted and sucked harder. Every suck and tug on her nipple brought more moisture out of her, until her arousal crawled down to her ass.

He squeezed one breast while sucking the other, but he didn't stop there. No. The amazing torture continued. He slid a hand down her body and managed to make his way between her legs. With a gentle flick, he rubbed a finger between her slick pussy folds.

"Oh good lord!"

He bit at her hard nub and she groaned. Then he flicked his tongue back and forth on her nipple at the same time he put pressure on her clit, rubbing the pleasure center in quick circular motions.

It couldn't be. He just started. How in the world— The speed and intensity of her orgasm caught her by surprise. She screamed loudly as she vibrated with the tidal wave of pleasure coursing through her body.

Her legs shook, bones feeling liquefied. There was no time to hesitate. He curled his arms around her large thighs, wrapping them around his waist. His hot, hard cock slipped between her folds, rubbing at her entrance and flirting with her girl parts. Oh yes. She moaned instantly. There was no way to hold back the throaty moan. Impossible. Not when her mind focused on how good he felt teasing her with what was coming.

He slid into her in a single powerful thrust. Deep. So deep she felt him stretch her muscles taut. And it felt so damn good. Like pleasure and pain and having a massage after a hard day of work. All kinds of decadent things.

"Oh!" The gasp tore from her throat at the same time he pulled back and plunged back in.

He kissed her lips, her jaw, her neck, licking repeatedly at the bend of her neck and throat.

"Charli," he grunted with ragged breaths.

"Barry, please. You feel so good," she panted out between his harsh thrusts. Every glide of his body into hers was like watching fireworks. She was amazed, enthralled, and wanting more.

"Ah, my beautiful temptress," his churned-gravel voice grated out. "You're so slick, hot, and tight." Her pussy fluttered tightly around his thickness. "I wish you understood how badly my bear and I want to keep you. To make you mine—ours." He met her gaze and didn't glance away. The possessive intent in his eyes warmed her insides to near a Florida-in-July type of hot.

"I want to keep you like this," he pressed his lips to her neck, his tongue flicking around her beating pulse. "Cuffed. Where you're mine for the taking. Day and night. I'll fuck you all the time and fill you with cum. Mine. Only mine, and nobody else could have you. That's what I want, beautiful. You. I want you chained to me for all fucking eternity," he snarled.

"Barry . . ."

"Say you want it too, Charli."

God, yes. She wanted to be his mate. But it was too soon to try to figure that out.

"Come on, sweetheart. Say the words. Tell me to keep you mine forever."

She swallowed at the dryness in her throat. "I . . ."

Another moan tore from her throat when he increased speed. He slammed his rock-hard cock into her. Again and again. There was no fight in her, only acceptance, need. Taking everything he wanted to give.

He thrust harder. He slipped a hand between their slick bodies, down to her pussy, and pressed on her pleasure nub. Wildfire heated her blood and scorched her veins. The tension in her core broke, shattering into a million breaths and heartbeats.

His lips crashed over hers. Her scream was drowned by their kiss. It went on forever, or for a few moments. She couldn't tell time any longer. Not that it mattered, when all she knew or cared to know was the pleasure he gave her. Keeping it going and enjoying every second of it. Her pussy gripped at his cock, contracting against his driving shaft.

Pleasure cascaded through each of her limbs. She tore her mouth away from him, gasping air into her burning lungs.

The cuffs came off and Charli flipped onto her belly, ass in the air. She gripped the bars, anticipation making it impossible for her to think straight.

"Fuck!" he snarled, thrusting his cock into her pussy from behind. He held her hips in a painful grip. With a quick glance over her shoulder, she watched him finger the lube and toy. Yeah, this was getting a lot more interesting. Their gazes met, and his feral look made her slick all over again.

With a single-minded thrust, he was in her, taking and owning her body. He reared back and drove deep. Again and again. He continued to fuck her like this was their last night on earth. Charli couldn't breathe, much less hold a thought. She gasped for air as each pummeling drive shoved it right back out of her lungs.

His fingers turned into claws at her hips, biting deep into her flesh. A rumble sounded from behind, like he was losing control of his own body. Damn if that wasn't sexy as hell.

The sole thought of him letting his wild side take over did something to her. It pushed her over the edge. She choked a cracked scream. Her muscles went from tense to loosening rapidly, riding the pleasure wave again while he plunged hard into her sex. His grip squeezed her hips hard, the pain mixing with the pleasure and heightening her experience.

She'd have wounds later, but that didn't faze her. She wanted this—him. More. Anything and everything he wanted to give. The claws tugged, scratching deeply, leaving bleeding marks as he came. His cock pulsed inside her, filling her with his seed.

Cool liquid slid down her ass. He was still hard inside her. Shifters had an unnatural ability to keep going multiple times without needing to rest. He rubbed a finger over her hole, dipping it into her and spreading the lube inside. In and out. He went on that way for long moments.

"I'm taking it, Charli. Tell me to do it, beautiful," he said in his barely human voice. "Tell me to fuck you in the ass."

Good god, he was a pervert. And worse than that, she loved the things he said. Obviously they were meant to be together.

"Give me the golden rabbit," she said, holding her hand out at her side.

He placed the vibe into her hand. It had a long see-through body. There were rotating beads inside, along with a bunny at the front for clitoral stimulation, and a powerful set of controls. She hadn't been with a man in years, but she had amazing adult toys to keep herself entertained.

Barry continued driving his finger into her ass, pushing in and out. She gasped and groaned.

"Relax, love. You're going to love this."

She'd done this before, so she knew it depended on the partner. So far Barry excelled where others had failed.

A second finger went in and he scissored them, stretching her. He continued to drive into her pussy while going in and out of her ass with his fingers. A third finger slid in and spread her at the same time he added more lube into the mix.

"That's it, baby. You're ready for me."

She moaned at how much she enjoyed pushing back into him. His cock slipped out of her and his digits left her to be replaced with his dick at the entrance to her asshole. Barry had lubed himself up well. She could tell by how easily he was gliding into her.

It was time to make things more interesting for herself. She pressed a button on the rabbit and rubbed it up and down her pussy. The soft buzzing helped shoot up her pleasure and take her mind away from his driving into her ass.

"Push out, sweetheart," he grunted. "Make it easier for me to get into your sweet ass."

He gripped her cheeks open, sliding into her with tiny seesaw motions. She pressed another button and the buzzing increased. She had the little bunny rubbing around her clit and slowly making her body tense. The vibration of the toy on her pussy sent her closer to the edge.

Before she knew it, he was fully inside her. He pulled back and plunged deep and fast.

"Ah, baby. You're so fucking tight!"

She whimpered, her breaths coming in sharp puffs of air. Blurriness crowded the edges of her vision. Her muscles tensed, readying for her impending climax.

She pressed her face into the blankets. Good god. She was so close. So fucking close she might pass out from how hard her body tensed. Her hand holding the toy shook. She didn't hold back any longer. She placed the toy directly on her clit, allowing the vibration to take her to heaven. Her ass squeezed at Barry's cock.

He growled, pumping faster into her. Her pussy grasped at nothing, looking for penetration. The tension ebbed away, leaving her filled with delight. Sight and sound ceased to exist. All she knew was the wave of pleasure pulling her under.

He grunted, slowing his thrusts. His cock felt like a hot bar sliding into her. Suddenly the bear roared. His hips jerked into her, his dick still pounding her from behind. He squeezed at her ass, pushing deeply into her and filling her with his cum.

She couldn't move. There was no way she'd move from there at all. Ever.

"Oh, Barry," she choked out.

"Relax, baby. We're just getting started."

What in the world had she gotten herself into?

CHAPTER SIXTEEN

Friday morning, Charli and Barry walked up the steps to the fellowship's front office door. "You ready for this?" she asked.

He shrugged. "As ready as any convicted felon can be."

She slapped his arm and frowned. "Stop with that. We don't have any, well, much evidence that you were involved with the armored truck wreck."

His brows drew down in a serious no-nonsense frown. "No, just the money."

Charli scowled. "Be positive for me, at least."

"After last night," he started, his lips suddenly lifting into a fuck-me-now grin, "I will do anything for you. Who knew the tiger in you liked being dominated? Even though you're not a shifter, baby, you are an animal under the sheets. Or out of them."

Charli blushed to her neck. She was definitely not known for her sexual prowess. But damn, last night was the most educational romp she'd ever had. The lube. Wow. She wanted to go home and do that thing all over again.

When they walked into the office, Devin was at his perfectly organized desk. He even had the same number of pens and pencils in his
black mesh holder. Charli didn't understand how Devin got anything
done with always having to put stuff back where it belonged. She'd
spend so much time straightening at the end of the day, she wouldn't get
back to the house until midnight. As long as she had an idea of which
side of the clinic the item was on, she was in good shape.

"Morning, Devin," she smiled at the panther. "Working on the
case so early?"

Devin sniffed and raised his brows. Heat crowded her cheeks.
Damn, could he tell they'd had sex? Nah. She'd showered.

"Morning, Charli, Barry. Yes, something about this whole no-
entrance, no-exit evidence is eating at me. But no worries. I'll figure
it out eventually." Devin seemed so calm. Nothing rattled him. She
needed whatever it was he was having for breakfast. Valium?

She set her purse in her bottom desk drawer. "Is Milkan in yet?"

Devin nodded, still fixing things around. "He came in not too
long ago and is in a good mood. If you want to ask for something, now
would be a good time."

She nodded, her heart filled with hope that the boss would be able
to help. "Perfect. Thanks."

The director's door opened and she looked up at him. Milkan saw
her and quickly stepped back into his office. Good, he recognized that
she wanted to talk with him. She told Barry to stay in her office while
she and Milkan talked. He shrugged and headed for Devin's desk.
Hopefully those two could talk shifter for a bit.

Charli knocked on her boss's door. "Milkan, do you have a minute?"

"Come on in, Avers. I figured you were here early for a reason," he
said with a genuine look of interest and what appeared to be concern.
She didn't know him well, so she wasn't sure what to make of him yet.

"Yes, sir." She cringed on her way in. "Sorry, sir. I mean, no sir."
Oh, for fuck's sake. She needed to get her shit together. "Well, I mean

Milkan with *no* sir." Good god, she was babbling. How afraid was she of his answer? She could lose the only man she ever cared for.

"It's okay, Avers. Whatever you need, I won't bite your head off. I'm not one of those bosses."

Charli smiled and relaxed. Maybe she would like working with this man. Either that or her need to ensure Barry's safety was making her want to be friendly with her boss.

"Thank you, s—Milkan." She took a seat and folded her hands in her lap. "I have a situation with Barry and I don't know what to do."

"What's the problem? He's not hurting you, is he?" Milkan looked ready to spring from his desk chair.

"No, no. Nothing like that." She inhaled a noisy breath. This was so not going the way she'd planned or hoped. "We . . . I think Barry may have something to do with the armored truck robbery yesterday."

The director's brows lowered. "Was he not with you yesterday? Isn't his memory gone or something?"

She nodded. "Yes, he had some form of head injury that I think caused it. We hope it won't be long term, but it's not looking to come back immediately."

Milkan pursed his lips. "Okay, let me know the moment he recalls anything. Especially if what you think about his involvement with the robbery turns out to be true. What part did he play?"

She scrunched her brows together. How to explain she had no real idea of what the hell was going on without sounding stupid? "It's really weird. When I found him under a bridge unloading orange bags of money, he was in a zombielike state. He didn't hear or see me when I called or touched him, at first."

Milkan's eyes widened. "Orange money bags? So he had the stolen money?"

She bit her lip and winced. "I'm not sure, but I think there's a distinct possibility they are one and the same, yes."

Milkan sat back in his chair and steepled his fingers under his chin. He stared out the window, silent. She'd wait for him to speak before giving more details. Her stomach churned. She was ready to throw up. He would toss Barry into jail without a second thought. How stupid was she to turn him in? But this was her job.

You care about him. Why would you tell on him?

Ugh. She needed some vodka-laced coffee.

In hindsight, she should've asked Devin or Russel to help prove his innocence, then brought everything to her boss. It was a good thing her duties in the fellowship dealt with the shifters' animal sides and not the human evidence. She'd suck at being a detective. Her specialty was really animals and talking to them.

The director leaned forward, resting his elbows on the desk. He didn't look happy. "We don't have much choice here, Avers. I think you need to keep him hidden for a while."

Charli opened her mouth, then closed it. What the hell? "Excuse me, sir. Keep him hidden?" That was nowhere near what she was expecting.

He raised a brow, his eyes void of emotion. "Would you like me to put him in police custody?"

"Oh no. Not at all. I was just prepared to, um . . ." How did she say *argue* without saying argue? "I was prepared to present alternatives, sir. I mean, no sir. I mean—"

He held up a hand. "I get it, Avers. You were going to argue. As I said, I'm not like most bosses. Keep him away from the police and the crime scene. Last thing we need is the media spotting him and starting to ask questions. Keep him with you and lie low until we get more information about the robbery from the police. As far as they think, at the moment, it's all human."

The director's intercom clicked on. "Director, Senator Hayseed is on the line for you." He pushed the com button. "Thank you, Sally." He released the button and wiped his hand over his face. "I hate talking to this prick. I haven't even had my second cup of coffee yet." He looked at Charli. "I need to take this. We'll talk later. Keep me updated on his memory." Charli stood and nodded, then left as the director answered his phone with a jovial tone.

She leaned against the wall outside the director's office. Her knees were nearly jelly. Barry was by her side in a heartbeat.

"Charli, what's wrong?" He brushed his fingers over her cheek.

Her stomach flip-flopped. Whoa, girl. She needed some distance or he'd know she had the raging hormones of a teenager on her first crush. She stepped away and laughed. "Nothing is wrong. I can't believe it. Milkan said for me to hide you."

Barry frowned, confusion clear in his features. "Hide me?"

"Yes. He wants to keep your involvement quiet. No police." Such relief raced through her that she felt light-headed. Barry put an arm around her shoulders and walked her to her cubed office.

"What else did he say?" He sat on the edge of her desk as she plopped into her chair. She met his gaze. A stray lock of hair had fallen over his brow and she brushed it away, instantly feeling an erotic pull to him. She saw his eyes brighten and shook her head. No way. Not at the office. "He didn't say much else. Oh, I forgot to tell him we left the money under the bridge."

"He didn't ask about it?" His lips pressed into a tight line. She wanted so badly to kiss away his concerns, but knew she couldn't. There was too much she didn't know, and she couldn't assume all was fine.

"No, that wasn't his biggest concern. He cared more for you. I think he's like no one I've ever worked for."

Barry sat quietly contemplating. "So what now?"

Charli sat back in her chair, her stomach still doing all kinds of weird stuff after the fear of losing him. "Good question. He's on the phone with some political big shot, so I didn't get the chance to ask."

She chewed on her upper lip. They needed to find out who Barry was. She couldn't go to the police for help, obviously. Who else had the equipment and access to online information?

Her face lit up. "I know exactly what to do." She snagged her purse from the drawer and stood. "Come with me. I'm taking you to meet one of my friends."

"Who's that?"

"She's a mad scientist with lots of high-tech toys."

His brows raised and a strained laugh rumbled from his chest. "Sounds like fun to me."

CHAPTER SEVENTEEN

Barry sat on the passenger side of Charli's SUV, heading down Interstate 5. The mountains west of them shone with the early sun. Snow-capped tips sparkled. A group of fowl flew overhead in a partial V formation. He thought it was late in the season to be moving south, but what did he know. Didn't bears hibernate?

Should he be sleeping somewhere? He knew exactly whose bed he wanted to spend the winter in. He stared out the window at the passing terrain. Who was this woman he'd come to care so much for in so little time? Fuck, he didn't even know who he was. What if he was married and had a family? Could he leave Charli to go back to those who depended on him?

He hadn't had on a ring, but being a shifter, that would be impractical. That was no help. The bear argued that he had no one but Charli. That she was theirs and there was no other. With how possessive the bear and Barry were of her, he worried he'd scare her. Thankfully, she never shied away from his domineering animal or whenever Barry reminded her that he wanted her for himself. To make her his mate. To keep her forever. She appeared to like that he wanted her. Thank god.

He couldn't imagine turning off the possessive bear or their desire to keep Charli as their own. *Mine.* The word drummed in his mind.

Take her. Nobody touches her. Fucking hell. This bear made life so damn difficult. He already had enough problems on his mind. Trying to figure out his past while feeling the need to protect and keep Charli as his own was turning into a full-time job.

Someone had to know who he was. Why hadn't anyone filed a missing persons report? He ran his fingers through his hair. Charli glanced at him.

"What's wrong?"

He let out a sigh. *Wrong?* He didn't know who he was. He wanted to have her stop the car and shove his face between her legs until she was moaning for him to fuck her. He'd been thinking of sliding between her silky thighs all fucking morning. Other than that, not much. "I was thinking about this mess with my memory, wondering why no one has made a claim on missing their—" He clamped his mouth shut, not wanting to admit to his words.

Charli looked away. "Missing their *husband*, right?"

Ah, fuck. He'd gone and done it. The scent of her fear and distress made the bear push at the human cage. He wanted out. Instead of letting the bear roam, he scooped her hand from the steering wheel and brought it to his lips. "Charli, whatever happens, we'll work it out." Dammit. He needed to stay in control.

He pushed the animal back and focused on ways to soothe his woman. No matter what happened, Charli was his. Of that, there was no doubt. "I'm not the man I was before the accident. I like you. I want to be with you more than you know. My bear and I, we are sure you're it, baby. And we want to make things work. You and me. You're it, Charli. I'm not going anywhere. This isn't going away." He waved a finger between him and her, showing "this" referred to their relationship.

She smiled, but he smelled her sadness. It created an intense ache in his chest to know he'd caused it. He hated her being so down when she had done so much for him. Changing the topic was probably the best way to go. "So, where are we going exactly?"

"It's the Fishing and Wildlife Service. I call it FAWS."

He grunted. "We're going fishing?"

A wide smile broke over her lips and he felt the air around them lighten again. "No, silly. It's the only place in the world dedicated to animal sciences and forensics."

"Animal forensics?" Was there really such a thing? "You mean like when animals commit a crime and you bring in the animal CSI team to handle it?"

She laughed and rolled her eyes. "Not exactly like that. More like testing blood to see if it's animal and what species. They inspect bullet wounds, stomach contents, bones, feathers, whatever to link crime scene, victim, and suspect. I'm sure they do more stuff, but that's the gist."

"And we're going there because . . ."

She huffed and fluttered her lashes at him. "Because I don't know what else to do right now. If there is anyone who could find out stuff about you, Marika is the woman. It's not like we can go to the police and have them research for us." She glanced at him like she was trying to hide a smile. He wondered what he was getting himself into.

The drive was peaceful. For some reason, he felt he hadn't had peace in his life for a long time. He got the feeling he didn't like his former self. Shit. What did that mean? If that was the case, then maybe he was a thief or some kind of criminal. That didn't sit well with him or his animal. The bear argued against it. It was still weird to have another being telling him what he thought. He was sure this was how people with multiple personalities felt.

They pulled into a parking lot outside a modern-looking white concrete building. Inside, Charli walked up to the reception desk and talked with the lady there. He looked at a framed aerial map of the area. Lots of trees and mountainous land with deep valleys that zigzagged for miles in areas.

Her clacking heels stopped behind him. "Just so you know, Marika is a bit . . ." She paused, which worried him.

"A bit what?"

A side door opened into the lobby and a high-pitched squeal echoed off the bare tile floor. "Charliiiii!" A short blonde with neon-green tennis shoes hurried toward them, arms spread wide. "Ohmigod! It's been forever." The woman stretched up and wrapped her arms around Charli's shoulders. "What brings you here? Another case?" She eyed him, then whispered to Charli, "If you brought him for me, I'll take him."

They both giggled. Barry couldn't help but watch them without saying a word. Seeing Charli with another female gave him a glimpse of her being more bubbly. They were clearly friends. She appeared to be very relaxed around the other woman.

"I know, right?" Charli whispered back. She straightened and cleared her throat. "Mari, this is Barry."

The bubbly blonde stuck her hand out to shake. "Hi, Barry. I'm single."

His cheeks warmed. Damn. He was sure women hadn't said anything like that to him at any point in his past. He took her hand. "Nice to meet you, Mari." His eyes darted toward Charli trying to refrain from laughing.

Mari bounced on her toes and clasped her hand in a clap. "Come to my office and we'll talk." She pivoted with a loud squeak from her shoe sole on the floor and power-walked toward the door.

He smiled. She was something else. He wondered how many Red Bulls she drank in a day, or an hour. "So, is she in charge of a three-ring circus or just drink a gallon of caffeine?"

"Stop," Charli slapped his arm. "She's a genius forensic zoologist studying shifter genomes, and a good friend. Not to mention helping us for free." They followed the path blazed by the overly perky lady.

Barry stepped from the hallway into Marika's office. His eyes popped wide; he'd swear an atomic paper bomb had exploded. There had to be ten trees' worth of paper scattered *everywhere*.

"Come in, come in, come in." Mari removed stacks of papers from what was slowly revealed to be a sofa. "Sit here, you two." She did the same for a matching upholstered chair. She sat with a plop, a huge smile on her face. "Would either of you like coffee?"

"No" immediately came from both of them. Just watching her buzz with energy was enough to make Barry jittery. While the two ladies talked personal chitchat, he stared at the whiteboard behind the office's owner. Symbols and numbers covered the shiny white surface, row after row. He now knew he wasn't a scientist or mathematician in his former life. The jumble meant nothing to him.

The women quieted and Mari looked over her shoulder at the board. Feeling like he'd been caught looking at nudie magazines by his mom, he tried to think of something to say. "That's quite interesting." He gave a chin pop toward the scribble.

Mari's face lit up more, if that was even possible. She hopped out of her chair. "You think so? One might think that the combining of inter-species hemoglobin would cause some sort of incompatibility hemolytic reaction along the lines of a disseminated intravascular coagulation. But maybe not. Sounds exciting, doesn't it?"

"Yeah," Barry mumbled. Holy shit, this chick was crazier than he was. He hadn't understood one word of that sentence, but he was sure he'd never been that amped. Even without remembering his past. Was this woman an enigma or what? Crazy, spazzy enigma. "Got it."

Next to him, Charli let out a bullshit cough. He scowled and looked at her. She patted her hand on his knee and winked at him. "So, Mari, we're hoping you can help us."

Mari fell into her chair, tripping over another stack of papers. "Oops." She straightened her lab coat and sat. "Absolutely—anything for a friend. Whatcha got?"

Charli looked at him. "Barry here has amnesia. Can't remember anything before hitting his head in an accident."

Mari clapped her hands together again. "Do you want me to probe his brain? We just got a new infrared tissue-imaging machine. I haven't had a chance to use it. You know how much I love power tools!"

Hell no. He wasn't about to become Dr. Frankenstein's next best friend. "Wait, what kind of probing are we talking about? The probe stays on the head side of the body, right?"

"If by head," Mari started, "you mean the one that holds earphones, then yes." She quickly added, "But if you want an anal probe, I can get Sam—"

Yeah, no. Not in this fucking lifetime.

"Nope," he cut in, "just making sure we are all on the same page, or body part."

Charli gave a soft chuckle. He could tell she was trying hard not to burst into laughter. "No, Mari. We probably won't need any probing. At least, not yet." She flashed an evil grin at him. "We need all of this on the down low. No police involvement."

Mari gestured to zip her lips closed and toss away the key. He wanted to burst out with a laugh. What were they, second graders?

Charli elbowed him, then continued. "He's a shifter, but believes he wasn't born a shifter."

Marika jumped to her feet and sucked in a scary breath. Her eyes widened and she made a surprised O with her lips.

"What?" both visitors exclaimed together. Mari whipped her head around to look at the whiteboard, then back around to them.

"That's what I'm doing. You said you got it?"

His cheeks warmed again. "Well, I didn't—I mean I—the letters—"

"Mari," Charli said, "I'm sure he got it, but you know, I'm just a veterinarian. So, could you explain to me?"

"Ugh"—Mari planted her fists on her hips—"you are so much more than just a *vet*, Charlynne Avers. Don't make me remind you what you can do that no one else in the world can."

"Ladies, please," Barry said in mock authority. He knew he wasn't in charge here. "Mari, tell us how your research relates to my situation."

She smiled as if she loved talking about her work. "I'm testing to see if human DNA and animal DNA can coexist."

"All that," Barry waved a hand at the board, "means you're meshing oil and milk?"

"Milk?" Charli asked. "What happened to oil and water?"

"I like milk better than water. Especially your skin."

Mari tilted her head. "Were you breastfed as a baby?"

"What?" Barry sputtered at her off-the-wall question. Charli laughed at his embarrassment. "Not that I remember. What's that got to do with anything?"

"Oh, nothing. I just always wondered if it was true what they said about adults who were breastfed versus those who weren't—"

"No," he broke into her whirling thoughts. "I don't want to know, whatever it is."

"Mari, why are you working on that? I thought you were into ancient animal genomes or something." Barry was grateful for her changing the subject.

"I was, until this project came in not too long ago. It's fascinating. And before you ask, it's classified, so I can't talk about it."

"But you already told us what it's about," Charli said, looking at the whiteboard. Marika stopped and seemed to ponder this.

"It's not the project that's a secret. Mainly where the data originally came from." She looked around as if looking for spies. "You didn't hear it from me, but aliens exist."

"Shifters exist." Charli shrugged. "Why not aliens?"

Mari bounced on her toes, giving another high squeal. "That's what I said. No wonder we're such good friends." She grabbed Charli's arm and dragged her to her feet. "Let's go to the lab and take some samples."

CHAPTER EIGHTEEN

Samples? That did not sound promising. Barry followed the women through a maze of halls to a door with a card reader. Mari patted the top pocket of her white lab coat, then the two side pockets. She turned in a circle as if she maybe dropped her ID badge. Barry tilted his chin to his chest to hide his rolling eyes. Whoever hooked up with her was in for a wild ride.

"Oh, here it is." From her pants pocket, she pulled out a plastic rectangle with her picture on it. With a beep, they were inside the laboratory. The large room was packed with a ton of stuff. Big machines, small machines, blender-looking things, glass vials—lots of vials. A lab technician stood next to a long counter watching a spinning gadget.

"Barry, have a seat here." Mari pulled out a desk chair in a small cove tucked to the side. "We'll start with your fingerprints. Make sure you're not an ax murderer wanted in ten states." Mari laughed, but Barry didn't as he caught Charli's frown. After a ton of ink somehow splattered the upper cabinets and smeared the countertop three feet on both sides of him, the lady closed the black pad and pulled out a set of vials.

"Okay, let's take a little blood for testing." Barry rolled up his sleeve, then Mari tied a stretchy band around his bicep. She spent the next five minutes digging through several cabinets around the lab. His hand had turned white before she returned. "Sorry. We have plenty of animal syringes, but only a few human."

She wiped a cotton ball soaked in disinfectant over the crease in his arm. Her chatter with Charli was constant and became background noise as he watched Mari work. When she picked up the needle, a chill ran down his back. He suddenly didn't feel well.

Needle taped on his arm, blood pumped into the vial—rich, dark blood. And more blood. Her fingers fumbled with another glass tube, and he felt the needle move in his vein as she held the filling vial. An *I'm going to be sick* shiver passed through his body. He realized then that she was going to attach another bloodsucking tube.

His head began to feel a little light. He stared at Charli instead of the blood leaving his body. He heard glass clink, then an "oops." A narrow stream of dark red fluid gracefully arced into the air in front of his face, then disappeared. The room started to spin, or it could be the chair. It did turn a full circle—no, that wouldn't be happening.

"Sorry, there. It's been a while since I've drawn blood from a living creature. With the dead animals, I just stick a needle in the leg, or shove a needle up an arm." The needle talk was only making this worse. His face felt cold.

"Other times, I jab the shit out of the body. Needle after needle after needle." Wait a second. He shook his head. Bad idea, the room tilted. Did she just say jab a needle over and over? Naw, she wouldn't say that. He had to be hearing things. He felt himself sliding down the chair as the world narrowed into black.

The last thing he heard before passing out was: "For a shifter, he sure is a wuss."

Something chilled lay on his forehead. It felt nice. Coldness seeped through his shirt and pants also. He certainly wasn't in Charli's bed where he wanted to be.

"All it takes is a swab for a quick probe." Sounded like Mari. "You just need to hold his cheek to the side while I stick it in, wiggle it around, then pull it out."

Swab, probing, ass cheek, in and out. Not happening. His eyes flew open with a holler erupting from his chest. Marika and Charli, leaning over his prone body, flew back from him, a yelp coming from each.

Charli sucked in a loud breath, hand over her heart. "Dammit, Barry. You scared the shit out of me." She and Marika laughed at each other.

He eyeballed the ginormous Q-tip in the researcher's hand. "What are you doing with that?"

Marika looked at her hand as if she'd forgotten what she was holding. "Oh yes. I need a cheek swab to go with the bloodwork. Say ahhhhh."

His body relaxed. This woman was going to give him a heart attack. "I thought you were going to stick that—never mind." Charli burst out laughing. She would get him and his thinking. *Mate.*

Mari stuck the piece of cotton on the end of a long stick between his gums and fleshy cheek, then yanked it out. "There we go. All done." She reached out her hand to help him up. For a little thing, she had strength that surprised him. She whipped him off the floor, then dropped him into the chair. He rolled backward until he bumped against a box.

"This is so exciting, Charli. Thanks for thinking of me."

"When it comes to forensics, you're my superwoman. We should do lunch or dinner soon. Do they ever let you out of here?"

She laughed. "It's more like: Do they ever make me go home?"

A ringing phone had Charli pulling her cell from her back pocket. She looked at the caller ID on the screen and frowned. "Avers here." Barry grinned at her tough investigator voice. "Be there in thirty." She tucked her phone into her pocket, then gave Mari a hug. "We need to go. Got stuff happening at the office. Thank you so much, Mari."

Barry stood to follow Charli. Mari waved. "Absolutely. I'm taking you up on dinner soon."

CHAPTER NINETEEN

C harli came through the door to Director Milkan's office after dropping off Barry and locking him in the cage. His choice, not hers. The cage. She hated it, but went with his decision. She'd given him her iPad for company at least.

She took a seat at the round conference table that had a propped-up computer tablet displaying the Shedford chief of police.

Director Milkan looked from her to the screen. "We're all here, Chief Charter. You can begin any time."

"Thank you, Director. Hello, Fellowship. Thank you for gathering so quickly. This case is still in the first forty-eight hours, and we hope to catch the killer before he can get too far."

"Any way we can help, just let us know," her boss said.

"I appreciate that, Milkan. Here's what we've got." A picture came into view of a beat-up and dented armored truck leaning against a tree, a creek flowing a few yards away. Charli froze in her seat. Her heart rate tripled. Devin and Russel looked at her, and she kicked herself for forgetting they could smell her. Sometimes shifters were damn creepy and a pain in the ass.

More pictures flashed on the screen, including the inside of the back of the vehicle. The guard lay on the floor, blood pooled around his head. The next photo was a close-up of the wound on the body's face and neck.

"Agent Avers." The chief said her name, snapping her out of a daze. "In your opinion, could these marks be the result of an animal, specifically a bear swipe?"

She put all thoughts from her mind, or she'd be all smelly again. "I'd have to examine the marks close up. Until then, I can't say for certain. I don't want to guess and send you on a wrong path. Why do you suspect a bear?"

Chief Charter held another photo to the web camera. It showed large paw prints in a muddy path leading to the creek next to bare human footprints. The shot screamed that a shifter had been there.

Director Milkan cleared his throat. "Any idea how the truck ended up at the bottom of the ravine, Chief?"

The picture went away to show the policeman's head tilted down as if looking at his desk. "Take a gander at this." He held up a shot of the road with black skid marks going off the side.

"We think something was in the road that made them swerve. Coming around the sharp corner in the outside lane, they would've been caught off guard and reacted instinctively by turning the wheel. What was in the road is anybody's guess. But it wasn't around when we showed up."

"Do you think," Milkan began, "a shifter is the culprit?"

Chief Charter glanced around with a deep scowl. "We're not saying that for sure, but the evidence shows there's a possibility. That's all."

"Understood," Milkan said with a sharp nod. "I agree with your assessment. I'll send one of my guys over to inspect what evidence you've collected, to see if it means anything to us."

Chief Charter flipped through pages in front of him and rubbed the side of his jaw. "That would be great, Director. I'll inform our front desk to buzz the detective in charge when he arrives." The tablet's screen turned black.

She glanced at Russel. She'd never seen such a grand smile on his lit-up face. The director stared at him. "Yes, Mayer. I'm putting you in charge of this case. But I'm warning you, she will put you on your ass if what I've seen so far holds true."

Russel's smiled never faltered. "No worries, boss man. I'll keep my paws to myself." She noted he didn't say *hands*. Men. That thought brought her hunky Barry to mind. She tried to keep calm, but the sadness tried to overtake her. She knew Barry was a good man, but that didn't stop what had already happened. She was going to lose him for something he didn't remember doing.

The men glanced at her again. Dammit. Let them fucking smell.

Milkan cleared his throat similar to earlier. "We're done here. Mayer, don't leave the building yet. I want a word with you." They all stood and pushed in their chairs. "Avers, do you have a minute?"

"Sure." After the two guys left the office, Milkan closed his office door and went to his desk. She sat in the same seat she had earlier that morning.

He clasped his hands on his desk and let out a sigh. "As you can see, we may have a problem."

Charli nodded, afraid to say something that could get her fired. She was a strong woman, but having your heart ripped from your chest would bring down the toughest person.

Milkan eyed her wearily. "I don't suppose any memories of his have come back since this morning."

She shook her head.

"Where is he now?"

Swallowing the lump in her throat, she told him about the cage and Barry's choice to stay in it.

Milkan sat back and sighed. "Do you think he did it?"

"I don't know what to think." She gazed out the window. The image of Barry grinning at her or talking to her added to her depression. He was a good guy. This was all wrong. "Based on what I know of him, I'd say no. But after finding him in the woods with that stash in the container and—"

"What stash?" The director frowned and sat forward in his chair. She realized she hadn't told him about their first finding yesterday.

She inhaled and let it out slowly, trying not to overwhelm herself. "Yesterday, we went back to where his last memory was and found a plastic container buried in the ground that had stacks of money and jewelry." Had that been only yesterday? It felt like days ago.

"What did you do with it?" Milkan's tone sharpened.

"Nothing. We had no reason to think it was anything more than someone's way to avoid banks. Folks around here do strange things sometimes."

Milkan got up from his chair. "Dammit, Avers. Take me to where this stash is. Could be evidence we need to break a case." He took a deep breath. "I'll follow you." She felt a little relieved he'd be driving his own truck. She didn't want to get yelled at any more than she had over this.

CHAPTER TWENTY

C harli slowed her SUV and parked along the side of the gravel road overlooking the creek and rockslide. Her boss parked behind her, then two more dark sedans stopped behind them. She met Milkan at his truck.

"Is that Chief Charter?" she asked as the cars' doors opened.

"Yes. He called and wanted to meet. I told him I couldn't and then had to tell him where we were headed. He insisted he and his team see this, too."

"Did you tell him it could be nothing? They could be wasting their time."

"I told him that. Apparently, he wanted to get out of the office on a Friday afternoon. He'll probably go home after this." The chief and Detective Gibbons walked up to them.

"Hello, Agent Avers, Director Milkan." The chief gestured to the lady next to him. "I believe you both met Detective Gibbons yesterday at a meeting."

"We did." Milkan shook her hand and Charli followed suit. "Good to see you again." Gibbons smiled and nodded.

Milkan turned to Charli. "We're all here, so lead the way, Agent." She led them up the hill and to the back of the brush pile. The only thing Charli saw was a hole in the ground where the container had been.

What the fuck? Shit! Fuck! Shit! This was not good. "It's gone. Damn it to hell. It was here yesterday afternoon." Who could've taken it? She remembered the shooter. Aw, crap! That must've been the owner protecting his retirement. After she and Barry had left, he probably took it home. It had to be. There was no other reason for them to get shot at. People in Shedford were very protective of their stuff, no matter where their personal items were located.

Charter squatted by the hole. "What exactly was in this box?"

Charli ran her fingers through her hair. Yeah, she was so getting fired now. No way to stop it after her clusterfuck involving everything from Barry to the money. She still wondered how the hell she'd gotten this job, but really she knew the answer. Her ability. Because there was no way in hell it was for her detective work. "There were several plastic bags of money. Jewelry was toward the side, but I don't know how much. The necklace Barry pulled out looked expensive as hell."

The chief looked up at her, his questioning gaze making her feel even more guilty over all she'd done wrong. "Who's Barry?"

She'd fucked up. Big time. "He's a friend of mine."

"You let a civilian tamper with evidence?" The chief got to his feet quickly and approached her, a menacing look on his face. Whoa there. This was not going to end well. If he even attempted to come into her personal space, he was going to be removing her from the case or arresting her, because she wasn't good at having anyone yell at her.

Milkan stepped in front of Charli. "My agent was with three friends when they stumbled upon the crate. They had no idea what they found. We don't know if it's evidence of some kind or a hillbilly's personal savings account."

The chief backed down grudgingly. "That may be the case. But when she said money and jewelry, the bank and jewelry store robberies came to mind."

She was so stupid. How had she not thought about that connection? Another reason for her to keep her day job. Crime details were not her forte. Charter turned to his men, giving them instructions to start their search for anything that could be a clue. He then called out, "Milkan, can I have a second with you?" He tilted his head toward the bottom of the hill.

"Yeah." Milkan put a hand on her shoulder. "Charli, is the bridge close by? Do you think the money is still there?"

She so did not want to answer that question. "I don't know. I assume it would be, but after this . . ."

He gave her a pat on the back. "Come down to the road with us." She and Milkan caught up with the chief and they made their way to the cars. Charter pulled her boss toward the last car. Charli checked her phone for messages.

A new e-mail had arrived an hour ago from her online scheduling app, which customers used to set up an appointment instead of calling. That was the most she knew about the social media craze and web technology. And she still preferred phone calls, but when taking this fellowship position, she had needed another way for folks to contact her.

Raised voices drew her attention. Her boss and Charter seemed to be in a heated debate. She hoped it wasn't over Barry. She couldn't let them take him from her. Really? Let them take him? She wasn't some dick-whipped woman in the throes of her first sexual experience. She'd known this man for only twenty-four hours. And had sex with him. More than once even! She had never been such a ho. But she'd never felt this way about anyone either. This was the second time, at least, that she'd admitted to herself how important he was to her.

But fuck. He could be a murderer and a thief. For all she knew, he could 100 percent be behind all these robberies. Hold up. That was ludicrous. Wasn't it? Maybe it was stupid, but she knew Barry. At least, she thought she did. Her instinct told her he wasn't capable of those robberies. That he was a good guy, and that even his bear's protectiveness of her spoke of the type of caring person he was. Her Barry was no criminal.

"Avers." Her boss called her over to him and Charter. There was a harshness in his voice she'd never heard before. He didn't look happy. She stopped next to the men. "Avers, I'm putting you on administrative leave until we get things figured out here."

Her jaw dropped open. "You're kidding, right?" When he didn't reply, anger boiled. This was her chance to protect her bear, and if they took her off the case, she wouldn't be able to do that. There was no way in hell she'd leave Barry defenseless. She was going to give Milkan more than just a piece of her mind. Milkan grabbed her by the arm and hauled her to her SUV.

He whispered to her, "Before you go ballistic, listen to me. You didn't do anything wrong in my book. I have to do this because Charter is here. I don't want him making a stink to others and blowing this out of proportion. It's only for a short time until he realizes there is nothing of importance in any of this."

Oh, maybe it wasn't as bad as it initially sounded. She knew she hadn't done anything wrong. Other than the obvious, but that was because she had yet to get the training she needed to better understand detective work. She'd been promised that training, and until she had the proper knowledge, she'd be used only to handle the animal side of things.

"Besides, you've been running in high gear since yesterday morning. Take a short break and enjoy your new boyfriend." He gave her a wink. "I want to go to the bridge, so don't leave yet. I'm getting rid of Charter now."

Charli pretended to stomp to her SUV, which released the little remaining anger she had at the situation. True to his word, Milkan talked Chief Charter into leaving, and with a smile on his face even. Damn, her boss was good. He climbed into his truck, and Charli took that to mean they were heading toward the evidence that damned the man she . . . liked a lot.

Where the creek crossed the road, Charli pulled to the side and got out of her truck. When peeking down from the upper bank, she didn't see the camo-green johnboat. Both relief and dread filled her. If the money was gone, then there was no evidence against Barry. On the other hand, if the money was gone, her boss might think she was a big looney toon and never trust her again.

"What do you see, Avers?"

"Nothing—literally." Together they descended the slope. Milkan looked around while she remained quiet.

"I see a partial footprint that's smeared. We won't get a useable impression from it. On the shelf, dirt and pebbles show evidence of something being dragged off recently. So I'd wager something was there."

He blew out a breath and ran his hand through his stubbly hair. "Okay, Avers. Go on home for the weekend. I'll call you later. You said Barry was locked in at your clinic?"

"Yeah, he didn't want anything to happen to him or anyone else. I have a pregnant cow coming to the clinic in half an hour, so I'll keep him busy with me."

"Keep a close eye on him, Charli. Don't let him hurt you. If he's innocent as you say, he has nothing to worry about."

That wasn't quite the truth. Barry still didn't have his memory. And he did have something to do with the armored truck robbery. But he had been locked in a cage all night, or with her. So the now-missing money bags were taken by someone else. She'd known for sure Barry wasn't guilty, but now the question was: Who was?

CHAPTER TWENTY-ONE

Before she did anything else, Charli went to the stall to let Barry out. She wouldn't have been able to talk to Mr. Harvey, one of her regular clients, without worrying about Barry. Now that she was home, he didn't need to be locked up.

"She looks good, Mr. Harvey." Charli stepped from the cattle stall where a cow with a loaded underside stood eating hay. "She's healthy, and the baby's growing well. I doubt she'll miscarry this time."

"Good. Pert near killed her last time," the old man said. "Let's get her in the trailer. I ain't had lunch yet and it's done past noon." Charli's stomach growled in response. He chuckled. "Soundin' like you hadn't either, young lady."

She sighed. "It's been a long day already for me."

"Yap, one a those. Have me some of 'em sometimes, too." He closed the trailer's gate and headed for the truck cab.

"Tell Maureen thanks for the pie. Blackberry is my favorite."

"Yap, that's why she made it. Knew I was comin' over. Call ya when she goes into labor." She was sure he meant the cow and not Maureen going into labor. She waved as he drove away. She cleaned up, eager to get to the house.

She opened the kitchen door to the aroma of red meat and spices. "Yum. Something smells good."

A deep growly voice greeted her. "It looks even better than it smells." He swept her into his arms, apron wrapped around his waist. "And you smell good enough to eat. Again."

Her face became burning hot. Barry laughed at her embarrassment. "You're so cute when you're mortified."

She slapped him on the arm and pulled away. "Is this for lunch? Steaks? I'm starving."

He picked up the platter with the meat and made a deep bow. "Your lunch will be ready momentarily, milady. How long are you home? Do you have to go back to the office today?"

She sighed, thinking back to Milkan granting her "vacation" time. "Actually, I'm off for a while. Well, until this situation with you and all the robberies is resolved."

She should be worried about being placed on leave, but the reality was she wanted more time with Barry, to get to know him. Helping him and seeing where things went with them wouldn't be a bad use of her time.

His brows lowered. "Wait. Are you suspended? Because of me?" He slammed the steaks on the center island, his face flooding red. "Those fucking bastards. They know you aren't doing anything wrong. Is it because of me?" Anger, sorrow, and pain mixed in his eyes. He dropped his chin to his chest.

For a second, she stood rooted to the spot. Barry, her Barry, was angry for her. People never worried about Charli. They never cared if she was dealing with too much or the problems that came with her job.

Not even her past boyfriends had bothered to ask about her animals. She loved that he cared about her, but she didn't like that he felt it was his fault.

She put her arms around his waist. "It's not because of you. Well, it is and it isn't. It's no big deal." Charli licked her lips, debating whether to say what she was thinking. "Besides, it means you and I will be here together all day and night for a while."

His head popped up, eyes twinkling. "I thought of that just as you said it. I love that you're so horny, my love." He cupped her ass cheek and pulled her against his growing hardness. "And I love that it's all because of me." Barry growled and set in on her neck with playful bites. She laughed and pushed away from his hold.

"Give me a break. I haven't had sex in a long, long time. I have a lot of time to make up for."

His grin widened. "I like the sound of that."

"All right, Mr. Hound Dog." She punched him in the arm. "I'm starving, so food comes first." She handed the steaks to him.

"But I'm having my way with you right after." He gave her a kiss and growled. "For an indeterminate amount of time." She followed him to the back porch where the grill was already heating. Off to the side sat her square card-playing table with two folding chairs fitted with throw pillows from the living room sofa. On the table, a basket of bread sat covered, and a handful of beautiful wildflowers stood in a glass jar filled with pea gravel and water.

"Barry, this is wonderful. The flowers are great. How did you know to decorate with colorful pebbles? Most men wouldn't have gone that far."

He shrugged and laughed. "Oh, I don't know. Figured I was a fancy designer before hitting my head."

She giggled and sat on one of the pillow-cushioned chairs. "I doubt that."

He set the plate with the steaks on the grill's little side table, then scooped her up from the chair and swung her in circles toward a huge tree.

Settling her on her feet under the far-reaching limbs, his hungry lips took hers. Desire heated her lower stomach. She felt her wetness slip out of her pussy onto her panties. A deep rumble vibrated her chest, coming from the gorgeous man beside her.

He pressed her against his rock-hard cock. "Fuck, baby. You smell so damn good. Screw the steaks. I'll eat you, one bite at a time, one lick at a time, until you come so hard on my face, you'll see stars." A shiver rolled through her body. She so wanted what he described. Hell, she was ready to throw down here on the ground.

Something hard, but light, fell on her head. She jerked back from Barry and looked up. "Tom, you have horrible timing." A squirrel perched on a branch overhead chattered noisily.

Barry frowned. "Who's Tom, and who are you talking to?"

Charli laughed and sat on the ground. "Are you jealous of a little squirrel?"

"Squirrel? You're talking to— Wait, more importantly, is he talking back?" Down the tree trunk two critters raced around and around until jumping to the ground and hopping to her sitting position.

"Yes, they talk back, in a way. They don't use their mouths like in the movies." She tore off small chunks of bread she held, which she'd grabbed from the table while she'd been sitting there. The little pieces were handed to the animals. They took them right from her hands.

"How do you talk to them?" He gave her a curious look, not the *you're fucking whacko* look she was used to.

She loved that he was genuinely interested in what she did. "I have to be in physical contact with them. Don't know why. That's just how it works. Then I hear words in my head or sometimes just pick up on feelings if the emotions are running high. It helps a lot when diagnosing illness and injuries."

"I'd say so. Just like a doctor asking the patient where it hurts." He went over and lifted the grill lid and placed the steaks on the searing metal grid. "I see why you're such a great veterinarian. You have insider trading secrets."

A few songbirds hopped along the ground next to her. She put out bread crumbs for them. "I guess you could call it that."

Barry set the plate and tongs next to the lid. "There is something I don't understand." He shifted his weight to his other foot. "Why would they start a unit with shifters and an animal whisperer here?"

She sighed and glanced at Barry's curious gaze. He was such a sweetheart. So ready to talk to her about anything. She knew her job was boring, but he appeared genuinely interested. She couldn't tell him how much she appreciated his making an effort to learn about her. "I asked the same question. Seems this area has the second-highest concentration of shifters and animal varieties of anywhere in the world."

"What's the first?" he asked.

She put more bread crumbs on the ground for the little critters she loved. "Shenandoah Valley, outside DC."

"Why there? That seems like a strange place."

A stillness came over the air suddenly. She glanced around her yard, trying to figure out what the cause was. "Don't know. That's what they told me."

Barry raised his nose into the air, sniffed, and a growl came from him. He lowered into a crouch and bared his teeth. Charli was on her feet instantly. "What is it, Barry? What do you smell?" She knew only a few things would put a bear on alert. And those things were all very bad.

CHAPTER
TWENTY-TWO

Barry's growl scared her. It was deep, loud, and ferocious. She'd never heard a bear make that kind of sound before. Charli hurried from beneath the tree onto the back porch and looked around, searching for anything out of the ordinary. Movement in the distance caught her eye.

From the woods on the other side of the yard, a coyote trotted out. Barry's snarl deepened. "Barry, no. It's okay. He's a friend. I helped him when he had a broken leg a while back. We talk occasionally." In fact, she had helped scores of wildlife in the area. Everything from setting broken bones to nursing baby birds left motherless. That was an educational experience. She learned she hated chopping up worms to feed to squawking open beaks.

She hurried toward the coyote before she had a pissed-off bear to deal with. She went to a knee and took his muzzle in her hands. She picked up on his fear right away. Not much frightened a coyote in this part of the woods. Just bears and humans. Charli focused on the animal's eyes, listening carefully.

Man.

What is the man doing? After a few seconds, she received images of dead animals with bleeding gunshot wounds. Was the human hunting? She wasn't sure why that would bother the coyote. They usually ran from hunters, and that was that.

Then she received images of her house and clinic from someplace in the woods. Like the coyote was at the edge, staring at her from a long distance.

Gun.

Everything snapped together quickly. She sprang to her feet and ran toward the porch. "Barry, get down!" He looked at her with a puzzled expression. "Get down, now!"

He lifted the grill lid and was about to ask why, when a bullet tinged off the grill's metal handle. "Shit!" He dove to the ground, a bit stunned. That shot would've killed him. Charli crawled across the porch. Another bullet splintered the railing in front of him, leaving a burst spindle. "Holy fuck!"

"Get behind the cooler, Barry. Keep something in front of you." He immediately sprang behind the long blue Igloo to the grill's side. She joined him, panting from her spent energy burst.

"What's going on?"

"The coyote saw a hunter in the woods, but he was setting up with my property in his sights." She slid on her stomach, careful to keep the cooler in front of her, to a metal container against the house that would normally hold garden tools and lawn stuff. She worked the combo lock, lifted the top enough to get her arm in, then pulled out her scope and rifle.

The grill's lid squeaked as if someone was lifting it. She whipped her head around to see a hand with a pair of tongs slide through the narrow opening to the meat.

She whispered loudly. "What the hell are you doing? You're gonna get shot."

He flipped both pieces of red meat. "These steaks are too good to let burn. And I'm starving." Another bullet ricocheted off the grill. His hands quickly disappeared, leaving the tongs lodged between the lid and side. Before she could reply about men and their grills, his hand snapped up and snatched out the tongs. A bullet sank into the house's siding by her head. She ducked lower and pulled out a Glock from the box.

He looked at her, licking his fingers. Not appearing overly concerned they were being shot at. "The animal just told you about this?"

She army-crawled to the cooler and handed him the Glock. "Sorta. He was too keyed up to talk, mostly. I got mainly images of what he saw."

"Did he show you a scene of the shooter's face?"

She scowled. "No. Didn't get that."

"Have you pissed off any of your neighbors lately? Or made a cow sick?" There was humor in his voice. Was he losing his mind, finding this whole thing funny?

"I don't make cows sick," she huffed.

He chuckled. "Sorry. You look cute trying to dodge bullets."

"Shut up and tell me what you hear with your supersonic ears."

"Oh yeah. Forgot about that. Being a shifter can be cool." His eyes closed and he held his breath. Charli stopped breathing, too. She heard nothing but the ringing in her ears from the bullets being shot at them. No squirrels, dogs, or crickets. Not even a breeze.

A flock of birds flew overhead, heading in the direction of the shooter. Charli hoped the shooter didn't get it in his head to shoot at the massive group. They disappeared into the trees. Seconds later, a noise came from the woods. She hit Barry on the arm and mouthed, "What do you hear?"

Barry grinned. "It sounds like all those birds are dropping bowel bombs on him. He's pissed as hell."

Bowel bombs? "You mean they are all pooping on him?"

He laughed and nodded. She was flabbergasted. How did they know to do that? Then a thought hit her. Could there be bird shifters? That seemed unlikely. Why would Mother Nature create something like that? A shot fired, but she didn't think it was at her and Barry. The birds scattered into the sky.

Charli aimed in the general direction of the shooter and sent out her own deadly gift. She didn't expect to hit him, but she could at least warn him to not come closer.

She had readied for another shot when the air suddenly filled with the howl of wolves and coyotes. The chilling sound started on one side of the woods and flowed to the other, like the wave during the seventh-inning stretch. Charli shivered in spite of having no fear of the animals.

Barry's hand touched her shoulder. "Wait. I hear a bunch of noise. Like the guy's shuffling through the leaves. He's going away, straight back." He moved so his head was above the cooler. "What's on the other side of the ridge directly ahead?"

"There's a highway in that direction. It's a national forest preserve, so there could be campsites, parking lots, trails somewhere." So the shooter could be anyone from anywhere. Like the other morning. She sucked in a sharp breath. "Barry, do you think he could be the same person who shot at us yesterday when we were checking on the plastic container?"

He thought for moment. "Could be, but I don't see how or why. If it was a local protecting his property, why would he be here? He couldn't have followed us. You'd think he took his stuff since you said the container was gone. He has no reason to be here."

He made good points. That idea was shot down. Who else would it be? And were they shooting at Barry only? Who would want him dead? Of course! Someone who knew his secret and didn't want him remembering.

The first coyote padded up to her and she put a hand on his neck to rub the soft fur. She focused on his eyes and one word came to her mind. *Safe*. She wondered if this coyote had gathered the wolves and others they heard wailing in the forest. That idea scared her, but calmed her also. If the critters in the area had her back, then she was much safer than she had ever thought.

"I think we're okay, Barry. The animals are saying he left."

He jumped straight up, tongs in hand. "Just in time. The steaks are done."

CHAPTER
TWENTY-THREE

Devin slumped on his desk, staring intently at his computer monitor. There had to be clues in the bank security footage of who the female robber was and how she got in and out of the building. There was a logical answer. He just had to find it.

Russel passed his desk area, stopped, and leaned back to peek at his screen. "Hey, dude. Is that the naked lady—I mean, the perp at the bank robbery?"

Devin sat back in his chair and stretched. "Yeah, been staring at it for thirty minutes and haven't seen squat."

Russel got a big grin on his face. "If you want, I'll take a look at her—I mean, the footage again and see what I see."

Devin stood from his chair, shaking his head. "The director was so right about you being a walking harassment case." He slapped a hand onto Russel's shoulder as the man slid into the chair in front of the computer. "But no worries, man. I'll be there to bail you out and laugh my ass off when Milkan chews you a new one."

"Thanks, man. Nice to know you got my back there." Sarcasm flowed in his words.

Devin leaned against the desk, watching Russel click Play on the footage. "Anytime. We're a team. Speaking of which, aren't you supposed to go to the police station about your case?"

"Was. Milkan called a little bit ago and said my beautiful Detective Gibbons wouldn't be in the office since she was with him and Avers. Guess it'll have to wait until next week. It's pretty late already today."

"What's up with you and Gibbons? Are you always a horn dog for a pretty woman, or is she special?"

Russel shrugged. "Was a horn dog, and yes."

"Was?" Devin raised a brow.

"Dude, she's my mate."

"But she's human." He frowned.

"Are you a speciesist?"

Devin barked out a laugh. "What the hell is that?"

"Dude, you're from LA and don't know what a speciesist is? Y'all probably tagged the term."

Devin rolled his eyes. "Yeah, whatever you think. Spit out the definition."

"It's someone who is prejudiced against humans or shifters—the species of this planet."

Devin rubbed a hand down his face. "I'm not a speciesist, Mayer. I dislike both in equal amounts."

Russel stopped the images on the monitor and turned to Devin. "Have you always been this happy-go-lucky or did the big city jade you?"

Devin shoved his hands into his pockets and stared at his cubical floor. "I don't remember always being this way. I used to be quite different."

"Different how?" Russel swiveled in the chair to face him.

Devin shrugged. "I was never as organized as I am now. In college, fifteen years ago, my dorm room was a disaster of papers and books. I could never find a pen to write with. Shit, I was lucky to know what day it was for which class to go to."

"Seriously?" Russel glanced at the black mesh pencil holder and the pens neatly packed inside. Binders and books were lined on a shelf by color and height. Every piece of paper was in a basket or folder easily found. "I couldn't imagine that."

"Yeah. When I was a rookie, I was so excited and loved what I did. I was almost bouncing on my toes ready to get to work."

Russel laughed. "That would be funny to see. You're so laid back and chilled all the time. What happened?"

He scowled and looked away. He didn't want to think about the incident that broke him. The incident that almost took his life, and he wished it would have. He let out a sigh. "Let's look at the security video. Maybe you can catch something I missed."

"I've got a better idea. We've looked at this video stuff before and didn't see anything. Let's check out the bank in person. Maybe we can pick up something there."

Devin pushed off the desk he leaned against. "Actually, I'd love to get out of the office. Should we call Director Milkan to see if he wants to meet us there?"

"Always a good idea to ask." Russel pulled out his phone and hit his speed dial button for his boss. It rang several times. He expected to get voice mail.

"What, goddamn it?"

Russel pulled the phone from his ear and gave Devin a questioning look. "Sir, Sonder and I are going to the bank to check on clues. Would you like to meet us there?"

"Sorry, Mayer. I didn't mean to yell at you. No, you two look around and see what's there. Update me on whatever you find. After that, go home. It's Friday. Not much more we can do."

"Yes, sir." He hung up before he got reprimanded for calling him sir. But when his boss was pissed about something, "sir" was the only name he was going to use.

CHAPTER
TWENTY-FOUR

Devin signaled his left turn into the bank parking lot. He and Russel waited in the middle lane for the massive trash truck to pull in first. The lot was filled with cars. The only open spots were toward the back corner. Being midmonth and a Friday, today would be a double whammy for employers with both salary and hourly workers.

From what Devin had seen since moving up here, most of the jobs were of the hourly status. Grocery cashiers, stockers. Restaurant staff. Hairdressers and the like. There were also professionals like a single law office or small doctor clinic housing a couple of general practitioners.

The smaller town was a drastic change. Going from Los Angeles to a population of just twenty thousand was almost a culture shock. He also had to get accustomed to friendly people who smiled and genuinely wanted to help others.

Russel opened the glass door to the bank and waved Devin in first. He looked around to see a line at the tellers' station wrapping around the lobby. Many others milled around the side areas where individual desks allowed for one-on-one consultations between banker and client.

He'd never seen a bank so full of people. If this was an example of how this particular day would go, he'd sign up for direct deposit through the department. He wondered if the armored truck robbery had anything to do with the mass?

Russel leaned toward him. "Who are we looking for?"

"The manager, Karen Bryde. Though I don't know how we're going to find her in here." A door to the side of the teller booths opened, and an older woman with her hair pulled into a high bun stepped out. She searched the area as if looking for someone. Devin headed her way, hoping she could at least help them if she wasn't who they were looking for.

Devin pulled out his badge from his sport coat inner pocket and flashed it for the lady. She smiled and held her hand out. "Agent Sonder, I'm Karen Bryde. I'm the manager of this bank. Thank you for calling ahead. As you see, today is a bit crazy around here."

"We noticed. We had no idea this went on."

"Only when midmonth is on Friday. Come back to my office. It's much quieter." The men followed her through the door. Devin recognized the hallway with doors on both sides. He looked toward the ceiling, straight ahead, and saw the security camera. This was the exit the thief would've taken to leave the bank, which, according to the footage, she hadn't.

The woman entered one of the offices and Devin smelled cat. Then he remembered the fluffy black cat they saw on the video. He slid his eyes toward Russel to see his reaction. Russel squished up his nose and frowned. Devin would've laughed if they were on their own.

Ms. Bryde gestured at the chairs on the other side of her desk. "Please, have a seat." She sat in a plush leather chair that reclined when she sat back. "How can I help you, Agents? The robbery has been four weeks to the day, and we've pretty much forgotten about it and moved on."

"Yes, Ms. Bryde, but the case remains open, and we're following up on leads and talking to those involved to see if anything more has come to mind that might be helpful."

"Of course, Agent. Would you like to see the vault?" She stood.

"That would be great." Devin grinned. "By the way, Agent Mayer here would love to meet your cat." Russel gave him the evil eye. "He's a cat person." Devin almost spit out a laugh.

Ms. Bryde smiled at Russel. A smile that took on an extra-friendly—maybe her attempt at sexy—look. "I'm a cat person, too, Agent. I have three I rescued from the pound at home. Snarky, the one that used to be here, isn't around anymore."

"Why is that?" Russel asked. Devin thought he noted a bit of fear in his coworker's eyes. He swallowed his laugh with a slight cough.

"We found her in the alley out back digging for food. Poor thing. We brought her in and fed her. She was so lovable. She'd follow me everywhere, always wanting to be petted or get a treat." She looked at the corner behind her desk. "I bought her a cat bed and she'd sleep all day. But after the robbery, she disappeared. I think all the police action, lights, and sirens scared her off." She sighed, then looked at the agents. "Shall we go?"

The men once again followed her down the hall. Russel stepped closer to Devin. "The day I pet a cat will be the day they cut my balls off because I'd no longer be a real man." Devin wanted to burst with laughter, but kept to his professional persona.

At the end of the hall where the camera attached to the ceiling was the entrance to the employees' break room. Aromas of Italian seasonings floated out. Devin's stomach growled. He was thinking carry-out would be good for dinner tonight. He stuck his head into the room to take a glance. To his surprise, the place was spotless.

"Wow, this place is immaculate. How do you do it with so many employees?"

Ms. Bryde laughed. "We don't. The cleaning lady just left. She does a great job for us. Without her, we'd look like slobs."

They turned the corner and saw the one door in this part of the building at the end of the hall. Devin noticed the camera aimed straight at the entrance. No way to get in or out without being seen. Ms. Bryde led them into the room containing the vault.

"Would you like me to open the vault for you, Agent?" Devin studied the room carefully.

"No, that's all right. What we're looking for doesn't involve the vault itself." He took in a deep breath, smelling nothing out of place. Just Ms. Bryde and faint cat. No other people. Maybe too much time had passed to smell the intruder. He searched the ceiling and walls for air outlets. A small white vent sat in the upper corner. That would explain the lack of smells.

Devin glanced at Russel. The man shrugged, signaling that he found nothing. Devin turned to the banker. "That's it for here, Ms. Bryde."

They left the room and Ms. Bryde turned down the main hall at the break room, but Devin stopped. He nodded in the direction where the hall from the vault room continued straight. "Where does the rest of this hall go?"

The bank manager turned. "That's a back aisle to the supply room and the alley on the side."

"May we take a look?"

"Sure. I need to check on the front. Are you all right by yourselves?"

"Absolutely. Thank you, Ms. Bryde."

The men pushed forward. The supply room was a tiny closet that didn't impress Devin. The reams of paper weren't stacked neatly. He heard a grind of metal on metal. Russel had opened the door leading to the alley. Both guys stuck their heads out to peep into the trashy, smelly area.

To the side of the door, a dumpster stood empty. Probably just dumped by the trash truck that pulled in right before they did. On the far end sat a homeless-looking man leaning against the wall. His head was down as if sleeping. Russel tapped his foot on the man's duct tape–wrapped sneaker. He looked up with one eye open. "Wha' you wan'?"

"What are you doing here? The bank usually isn't where folks hang out."

The man's face was rough. Deeply etched lines radiated from his mouth and the sides of his eyes. His salt-and-pepper beard looked like a rat's nest.

"Sometime, the woman give me the fancy food them bankers don't eat. Real good eatin' then."

"The bank manager gives you food?" Duh, Devin thought after he asked. If she feeds the cat, why not the homeless, too?

"No," the man grumped, "that uppty bish call cops on me. The lady with the snake eyes give me food. She scary. But gives me food, so . . ." He shrugged, then gave the deep, wet cough of a longtime smoker. Like his lung tissue was grinding down with each breath.

Devin squatted and looked the man in the eye. "What lady, buddy? Does she work in the bank?"

"Naw." He panted from his cough. "The cleanin' lady. She dumps trash an' bring me food if'n I here."

"Oh." Disappointed, Devin stood. He'd thought they were getting a break on the case. He sighed. "Thanks, man. You know there's a new shelter on Ash and Taft. They serve hot meals to those needing one."

The man looked at him with one eye open. "Ash an' Taft, huh?" He nodded until his chin rested on his chest. "Hafta check dat out, sometime."

Devin and Russel left their cards with the manager in case she needed to reach them and left. But something scratched at Devin's brain. Something that would blow this case wide open. What the hell it was, he had to figure out.

CHAPTER
TWENTY-FIVE

B arry struggled with his emotions. He went from everything being under control and getting shot not being such a big deal, to stressed out with concern for his mate. As it was, it was hard to control this emotional rollercoaster. Like his bear was fine and suddenly no longer in control of what was going on inside him.

He was happy to be with Charli, but sad they weren't "together" yet. Fear of Charli dying almost crippled him mentally. Anger coursed through his veins at the shooter for trying to hurt her. His bear roared at that. He took in a slow breath.

It was obvious to him that he had brought this danger to Charli. Before they met, she took care of cows, for chrissake. How dangerous could a cow be? Maybe if he went away, the trouble would follow him and leave Charli alone.

His hands fisted then relaxed, fisted then relaxed. He was pissed at himself for not remembering what had to be in his head. Memories couldn't be erased. They were there forever. Who was he that he brought this kind of danger to Charli? If he could only fucking remember. His fist slammed against his thigh.

Frustration took over everything. He wanted to go outside and claw at a tree. The image had his fingers shifting seamlessly into his giant bear claws. It didn't matter how much he tried to calm his bear down, the angry huffs couldn't be quieted.

Why, why, why? Maybe there was a reason he didn't remember his past. Could he have been such a horrible person that something was keeping him from knowing? He could be a serial killer, seriously. He could've gone insane and his mind snapped, leaving him a second personality. Insanity caused lots of shit, right? What if it was better to not know? To start fresh and keep his mate away from whatever he used to be?

But if he was so bad, why hadn't anyone reported him? Did they not know his identity? It's like he never existed before this.

He felt so fucking useless, and that only made the bear want to come out even more. The damn bear in his head confused more than helped. He had the overwhelming urge to protect Charli, keep her safe no matter what. The animal agreed, but what good did that do? Besides smelling, hearing, and healing, what was the fucking point? What was the purpose of that half of his soul?

No, he wouldn't believe what Charli had said about him. He *was* born human, one soul, one body. But why did he think this? He had no proof. More of a gut feeling than anything.

Exasperation was getting the better of him. Why couldn't he remember his past? Why was there an animal in his brain? Who wanted him dead and why? So many questions, but not one fucking answer.

He did know he loved Charli. So much so that leaving her may be his only option. It would tear his heart from his body, but if she died, he'd do much worse to his body. He was inadequate as a human and animal. Failing to keep his mate safe. They were always running. What kind of pansy-ass bear runs? *One that wants to stay alive.*

How fun is it to be alive if you can't live with yourself for being so pathetic? You'd think for someone without a past, no baggage tagging along, life would be great. Fuck that shit. He might have no past, but his present sucked. Unless he could figure shit out, he would only keep wondering about himself.

Charli glanced at him. "What's wrong, Barry?"

"Besides the normal stuff, nothing."

She gave him a soft smile. "We'll get through this."

"I'm not so sure about that."

"What do you mean?" The dread in her voice killed him. Could he say it? "Charli, I think—"

"Don't you fucking say you're quitting on us. I will be so goddamn mad at you. We haven't come this far just to—"

Her words pulled a grin from him. "Charli, 'this far' has been less than two days."

"So? Time means nothing, Barry. It's what's in here that counts." Her hand rested on her chest. She sighed. "Don't you get it? Stop being a typical man and listen for a minute." He couldn't help but grin at that. She was fiercely independent. He loved that about her.

She continued. "It has been almost two days. *Two* days. What can be solved in less than two days? Who stole the last cookie at the office? Who took your pudding from the lunchroom fridge? I hate that, by the way. The pudding is mine. Don't forget it." She smiled, which made him grin again.

She was so beautiful. How could he live without her? Life could be damn cruel.

"I can't believe how lucky I am to have found you."

She grinned. "If I recall correctly, I saw you first. Finders keepers and all that."

"Yeah, but . . ." he turned toward the window.

"But what, Barry? Tell me."

He let out a frustrated sigh. "I can't protect you, Charli. I can't keep you safe."

"What?" She sounded incredulous. "Are you serious? You're having a meltdown because you can't stuff me into a windowless room with padded walls forever? I'm not your responsibility, Barry."

"Yes, you are. You're *mine*." He saw the scowl on her face. Oh shit. He shouldn't have said that last bit.

"I'm *yours*?" She took a breath. "Am I some lousy piece of property you think you can own and tell me what to do?" Barry opened his mouth to apologize. She stuck a finger in his face. "No, you don't get to talk yet. I'm not done chewing you a new one."

He sat back in his seat. He deserved this for that comment. Charli began, "If I wanted your protection, I would ask for it. Who put your bare ass on the floor yesterday in two seconds?"

He held up a finger to interrupt. "I do believe my ass was in the air. My balls were on the floor and very cold for those ten seconds."

"Yeah, yeah. Be glad I let you keep them."

He grinned. "I think you might be a little glad, too. The way your tongue slides over them, and when you suck them into your mouth . . . Damn, baby. I'm getting hard thinking about it."

Charli slapped him on the arm. "Stop that. I'm trying to be serious. You're making it hard."

"I'm not the one making it hard—you are." He wiggled his hips. "All for you, baby." Charli busted out in a laugh. His heart soared with the sound. Could he give up listening to her voice, seeing her beautiful face every morning waking, and going to sleep at night?

Then a thought slapped him across the face. He was an adult and could do whatever the fuck he wanted. Some coward shooter shouldn't scare him away from what he loved the most. Why should an unknown past keep his future on hold? If he wanted to protect his mate, then he would; he just wouldn't tell her. And do a damn good job of it from now on. Unless . . . this whole thing was his fault. What if she was better off if he disappeared? Would her life be safer? Would she be happier?

No!

The bear refused to even consider it for a second. The man wondered if maybe he'd ensure her safety by getting out of her life.

CHAPTER TWENTY-SIX

Russel sat in the passenger seat of Devin's car, headed back to the office from the bank robbery site. Devin was pensive. Too pensive. Russel worried if his coworker remembered he was driving.

"Hey," Russel said, "you doing anything this weekend?"

Devin snapped out of his little world. "Um, not really. I'm still pretty new here. Don't know what's going on around town."

Russel snorted. "I take it you're not married or have kids."

Devin paled, and for a second Russel thought he might pass out. "Nah, man. I wouldn't know what to do with a woman if she fell into my lap. I try to stay away from that stuff."

Russel couldn't believe what he heard. "Don't you want to find your mate and have lots of bambinos?"

Devin glanced at him, then back to the road. "What's 'bambino' mean?"

"It's Italian for kids, babies. I know a few words in Italian, but mostly it's Greek to me." Russel waited to see if Devin would get his joke. Just as he was going to explain, Devin held his hand up, stopping him.

"Yes, dude. I get it. Greek and Italian. That's actually funny." No laughter or smile from Devin.

Boy, this guy was more than a bit weird. It would take Russel some time to figure him out. First lesson, don't make jokes when he comes out of his own world. "So, you have family up here or something? Not sure if I would choose Shedford over LA. Talk about opposites."

"That's why I moved up here. Opposites. It was time for me to leave the big city. When I heard about this group, I jumped at the chance. What about you?"

"We're from Seattle. Not too far from here. I go home twice a month so Mom knows I'm alive. She's so worried I'm going to get shot and die. She's human, so she doesn't get the whole *thou art shifter and hard as hell to kill* thing."

Devin nodded. "How did you hear about the fellowship up there?"

"My captain told me about it. Not sure why they asked me to join. Maybe all the other shifters said no and that left me. It was time for a change. Time for a move." Actually, he'd never wondered why they asked him. He was happy to do whatever they wanted. A new place meant new friends. And in his mind, the more, the merrier.

"What all has snake eyes?" Devin asked.

Russel looked at his coworker, wondering where his mind was. Was he all work and no play? Aww, man. He hoped not. He wanted get-togethers and parties. His family never needed a real reason to have a gathering. His baby cousin Tommy made his first shift as an infant, and his parents had everyone over for a cookout.

Russel reattached his brain for thinking, already in weekend mode. "Well, what kind?"

"What do you mean, what kind?"

"Snake eyes in Vegas are different than rattlesnake eyes in the woods." That was pretty funny, and he wasn't even trying with that one.

Devin frowned. "Animals, not dice."

"Ah, of course. Well, you got your reptiles: alligators, crocodiles. I avoid those, especially in a tasty form. Luckily they aren't this far north. I think fox, or is it foxes. Is foxes a word? It's like fish and fishes. Fishes used to not be a word, but I thought I read where it was now okay to use—"

Devin tensed in his seat and slammed on the brakes. "Cat!" he yelled.

Russel nodded. "Yup, cat would, too, depending on—"

"No. I mean there's a cat in the road."

Through the windshield, the fluffy black critter stared at Russel as its eyes turned from brown with round pupils to green slits. "Like that." He pointed. "They look like snake eyes now." A shudder rippled through him. "Damn furry monsters. What were the gods thinking putting those things on the planet?"

Devin lifted his right hand from the steering wheel and whipped out his slender razor claws. "You were saying?"

Russel let out a squeak. "Man, stop that shit." He batted at the panther paw as Devin laughed. "You know I don't mean *you* when I say 'cat.' I'm talking about those things." He nodded toward the four-legged creature that had resumed crossing the road, then turned down the alley between the water utility building and a clothing store.

"Oh shit, that reminds me," Russel groaned.

"What?"

"I need to pay my water bill before they cut me off. For some reason the bill didn't make it to my apartment, and I didn't think about it. I pay stuff when it comes in the mail. If they don't send me a bill, then as far as I'm concerned, I don't owe anything."

Devin chuckled and shook his head. "Mayer, it doesn't work that way. The world will rejoice when you mate. She'll straighten you out quickly, or you'll have a sore ass for a long time."

"No way, José. She'll have the sore ass after I'm done with her—"

"Mayer," Devin said between laughs, "TMI, man. Keep that shit in your own head. I don't want to imagine you and whoever in your apartment, buried in crap."

He gasped. "Fuck, you're right, dude."

"About what?" Devin asked with raised brows.

"I need someone to clean my place before she comes over. I think there's green stuff growing in the toilet."

Devin scrunched his nose in distaste. "That's disgusting. Do you ever clean it?"

"When it gets that bad, I just move to another place." Russel slapped his shoulder. "Just kidding, man. I don't sit on that toilet."

Devin roared in laughter. "Mayer, you're hopeless. If you really want a service to clean your place, call Bryde at the bank for who they use. She's very fond of cat people like you."

"Not doing it. I'll call the jewelry shop. I saw the lady there. She looked honest, from a distance at least. Didn't get close enough to smell her."

"Do you make it a habit to sniff women in public places?" Devin teased him. "I think I arrested you once in LA, in the park. You had a long overcoat on."

"Stop it, man. It wasn't you who arrested me."

Again, Devin laughed, caught off guard by his wild comebacks.

Russel googled the jewelry store for the phone link. He needed someone fast if he wanted to get his mate to his place this weekend. He was transferred to their office manager who gladly gave him the name of their cleaning service. He wrote it down and repeated it back to her.

After he hung up, Devin said, "That address is right around the corner. You want to check the place out? Get a feel for how reputable they are?"

"Yeah, if it's that close. Maybe I can talk to someone there and schedule a job on the spot. That'd be cool."

At the next light, Devin turned and took the first left. They pulled into an industrial warehouse park with rows of metal buildings with docks for loading and unloading cargo. They counted up address numerals until they reached what Russel wrote on his scrap of paper.

"Is that it?" Devin asked. They stared at a small, run-down aluminum structure. Dandelions grew through cracks in the concrete in front of the glass door that was padlocked shut.

"It's what she said she had on file. Maybe they moved and didn't tell her." The two windows were crusted with so much dirt and dust, they couldn't see in, even when they put their noses against the glass to peek. "Should we knock and go in?" Russel asked.

"I don't know," Devin said. "This thick-ass chain around the door says a lot."

"Well, that sucks. Let me try the cleaning company's phone number." The line rang until a voice said to leave a message and they would get back to him as soon as possible. "Right." He pushed the red button on his mobile phone.

Devin felt around the pockets in his sport coat and pulled out a few business cards. He shuffled through them and handed one to Russel. "What's this?"

"It's for the bank. Ask them who their cleaning lady was. You really need to not screw up things with your mate. One whiff and . . . whoo." Devin waved his hand in front of his nose as if fanning away an awful smell.

"Hey," Russel started, "I'll have you know I use air freshener."

"How often?"

"Whenever it gets bad enough that even I can smell it." Russel smiled and dialed the number on the card. Ms. Bryde gladly shared the information Russel was looking for. She highly recommended the lady. Russel hung up the phone and turned to Devin.

"You're not going to believe this. It's the same company and address the jeweler uses." He laid his head against the building's window. "Shit.

Maybe the neighbor girl will clean my place if I pay her a hundred bucks."

"Damn, man. I'd almost do it for that much." Russel looked at him with hope in his eyes. "I said *almost*."

Russel ran a hand through his hair. "Now what?"

Devin put his nose to the edge of the door where it met the metal frame. "I smell a lot of distressed emotions inside." He stepped back. "What do you smell?"

Russel breathed deeply against the slot. "Yeah, I get the same. Along with cat." With a huff, he backed away. "What is it with all the fucking cats suddenly? I don't have to mess with any for weeks, then—bam!—I get them all day long."

Devin stared at the door. "What if the lady is inside and she's hurt or sick? What if she needs help but can't reach a phone?" He looked at Russel and grinned. "I think we should go in just to make sure she's all right."

"You got it, boss." Russel lifted the heavy chain and wedged his fingers into a link, then pried it apart enough to slip off. With a lockpick tool Devin kept in his car, they made their way inside.

"Ugh." Russel pinched his nose closed. "This place is worse than mine." The front room wasn't much bigger than a box, with a file cabinet, desk, chair, and enough office supplies to make it look functional. The untouched layers of dust gave away the last time it was used as such.

After opening another door, they walked into the meat of the place. It resembled a frat house the morning after a big party. Pizza boxes, some with half a pizza remaining, were scattered around, along with Chinese take-out boxes, candy bar wrappers, soft drink cans, and general trash.

"Man," Russel started, "I would've moved out of here a long time ago."

"Nice to see you have standards," Devin teased.

"Whatever, dude. This is just disgusting. How can a cleaning lady be so . . . unclean?"

Devin shrugged. "You know the saying: the cobbler's children never have shoes." Next to a small door, several cleaning bottles sat in a tote along with a fairly new vacuum cleaner and brooms. "She has the tools of the trade. And they look like they haven't been used that long. Did you by chance ask how long she'd been working for either company?"

"Nope, wasn't too concerned at the time." Russel kicked trash aside to make a pathway toward a corner where several blankets were bunched on the floor. A pillow lay to the side. After a breath, he said, "This is where a cat sleeps. But what about the woman?" He looked around for a bed or couch.

"Maybe she sleeps somewhere else and just keeps her trash here." Devin smirked. "Maybe the cat is here to keep the mice away."

He noted a pair of hiking boots with mud stuck between the logo lines on the sole. A crumpled leaf lay nearby.

Devin said, "I didn't see a vehicle outside. Where do you suppose she is since her cleaning stuff is here?"

"I don't know," Russel began. "I get the feeling this cleaning lady isn't a real business."

Devin opened a door into a small bathroom. "Maybe it's a second job for her. Something she moonlights by herself."

"That's possible, I guess. But I'd rather bribe the neighbor girls with money. Safer."

"I hear ya," Devin said. "Let's go."

CHAPTER TWENTY-SEVEN

At the fellowship's office, Russel researched the cleaning company's name to see what he could find. The search engine returned 1.4 million results in half a second. "Shit. This isn't going to work either." He added Shedford to the search terms and came up empty.

"Well, slap my ass and call me Sally." This was getting irritating. He had to find someone else. "Hey, Sonder. I'll raise it to one fifty." He waited for a reply. Nothing. He knew Sonder was at his desk, even though he couldn't see around the cubical walls. "Sonder." He stood and looked over the beige plastic wall. Devin sat at his desk, staring at the jewelry security footage. Russel wadded a piece of paper to throw into his space. Something out of place would get his attention.

Russel launched the ball. Devin spun in his chair, caught it, and slammed it in the trash can. "Two points for me and an assist for you, boy." Russel should've known their extra strong shifter hearing would ruin any surprise attack.

"What are you so serious about over there? You were like this in the SUV coming here."

"It's on the tip of my brain. If I could just grab it."

"Grab what?"

"The answer to this case. I have it right there . . ." He closed his eyes for a moment, then swung around in the chair. "Dammit."

"You're thinking too hard, man. You can't do that. It's gotta come naturally when it wants, not when you want."

He spun toward Russel. "Get Detective Gibbons on the phone."

Russel's face lit up. "Now you're talking." He pulled out his cell and pushed the speed dial button for her that he had programmed earlier in the day. Devin came to his desk. A sweet voice filled his ear.

"Gibbons here."

"Hey, babe. Whatcha wear—" Devin grabbed the phone.

"Sorry 'bout that, Detective Gibbons. It's hard to turn him off, sometimes." He grinned at Russel. Russel flipped him the bird. Devin smiled.

Yeah, he and Devin would work out just fine. The guy may come across as weird occasionally. But honestly, who didn't in this day and age. Being a little psycho was normal. Even for a cat.

"Got it. Thank you, Detective. Have a good weekend." Russel grabbed the phone, wanting to talk to his mate before she hung up. Too late.

"Dammit, Sonder. I wanted to talk to her."

"She didn't want to talk with you. She called you an egotistical ass."

Russel flopped into his chair, a huge grin on his face. "She likes me."

Devin's brows lowered. "I said she called you an ass. How do you get *she likes you* from that?"

"Man, you just gotta know how women work."

"You"—Devin raised his brows—"know how women work?" Russel twirled his chair and propped his feet up on the side of his desk. He leaned back, fingers intertwined behind his head.

"Growing up between my sisters, their friends, my ten female cousins, and Mom and her friends, it's a wonder I'm not gay."

"Ah," Devin said. "That explains a lot."

"I'm going to ignore that remark, cat." Russel grimaced, feigning anger. "Anyway, I've seen all the games, all the mind fucks, and not-so mind fucks—and holy shit, the sexual escapades of some of them girls were hot. After eavesdropping, my inexperienced kid body had to go to the bathroom and spank the monkey a few times, if you know what I mean."

Devin stared at him for a minute with a puzzled look on his face. He opened his mouth, closed it, then opened it again. "Has anyone told you that you might be overfriendly?"

"Nope. When all the aunts and uncles bring the kids for a cookout, I'm one of the quieter ones. With all the females, I can't get a word in edgewise. But listening to them is better than a girly magazine. Shoowee. Well, until Mom talks. I just can't picture her and Dad in bed." He gave a whole-body wiggle. "That's just not right."

He continued. "Anyway, what else did my luscious mate have to say?"

"Yeah." Devon shook his head as if coming out of a daze called Russel's World. "Detective Gibbons, right. I asked her about fingerprints on the jewelry case since I didn't see it in the disaster box of files they sent over. There had to be one in all that mess." Devin parked his ass on Russel's desk next to his feet. "Listen to this.

"Gibbons said there were no prints except for a partial on a light switch. She'd forgotten about it, thinking it must've been tagged wrong because of what they got back. It took a while, but results said it belongs to a woman in DC who went missing six months ago. Her case is unsolved. Gibbons gave me a phone number for our branch in DC who dealt with the case. I think we should call them."

Russel leaned forward in his chair and brought his feet to the floor. "Absolutely, if you think they are still in the office over there." He dragged the desk speakerphone closer.

"If they are anything like the guys I worked with, they are never off duty. We take the job home."

Russel grunted. "I hear you, man. What's the number?" Devin rattled it off from memory and Russel dialed. After a couple of rings, a deep voice came through the speaker.

"Wheeler here."

"Director Wheeler, this is Devin Sonder and Russel Mayer from the fellowship in Oregon. How are you this evening?"

"Hey, great to hear from our first branch. All is good here. How about out there?"

"Not bad. We're getting set up. Sticking our toes in the water with our first big case, which happens to have a tie with your group."

"Really? What can we help you with? Hold on. I'm putting you on speaker so the agents in my office can hear, too." After clicks and some scuffing, Wheeler's voice came through sounding tinny. "Devin, you there? Or did I manage to hang up on you like I normally do with this damn high-tech phone crap?" Laughter came across the line.

Devin smiled. "Still here. Can't get rid of us that easily."

"That's a good thing," Wheeler said. "Whatcha got for us?"

"A bit of a mystery case. A set of prints for our thief here came back as a missing person from your area. Report shows it's unsolved. Her name is Melody Harpin." Voices rumbled in the background.

"Devin, we remember her case. She was in jail for DUI. Supposedly her husband bailed her out and two weeks later the department received a missing persons report on her. After nosing around, police found out she wasn't married. So whoever she went with when leaving, she must've known. Her apartment at the time hinted at a fight, with a lamp knocked over, furniture out of place, and a bloodstain on the floor."

"Was she a shifter?" Devin asked.

"No, normal human."

Russel asked, "Did she have a job?" Voices once again chattered in the background.

"She was a data manager at a local utility company."

Russel and Devon looked at each other. Both shrugged. Russel leaned closer to the speaker. "What does a data manager do, exactly?"

"Hi, Agents Mayer and Sonder. I'm Jane Ramirez. I was lead on that case. Ms. Harpin was a thirty-five-year-old female. Her one friend, also a coworker, said she was usually quiet, very unassuming, but friendly. No enemies, no family we could find. No previous arrests.

"Her other coworkers said the same. Supposedly, she was very good at what she did. Apparently, utility companies use a proprietary software to keep track of all their customers and consumption info. She analyzes all the data to spot trends for seasonal depletion, sees where usage is high or low for scheduling maintenance, and makes sure there are no ghost clients."

Both Russel and Devin said, "Ghost clients?"

"Yeah, not ghost as in *boo*, but clients that get lost in the system who aren't paying, yet are still using water, or those who are paying and saying they discontinued service. That kind of thing."

"Got it," Devin said. "Anything else that might help?"

"That seems to be all we have on her. Not much here. If you wanted someone who would hardly be missed by anybody, she would be a good person."

Russel thought that was interesting, as did Devin by his contemplative expression. Russel sat back. "Thank you, Jane and Director Wheeler. You've been a wealth of information. Y'all have a great weekend."

"Good luck with the case," Wheeler said, "and let us know if you come across anything that we can use to close the file here."

"Will do." Russel pushed the speaker button on the phone to disconnect.

CHAPTER TWENTY-EIGHT

B arry stared out the window as Charli drove them through the mountains and valleys, headed toward town. He glanced at her, her eyes focusing on the twisting road ahead. How much of that focus was on driving and how much was simply avoiding him? Her eyes went to the rearview mirror, then back to the road. The hilly two-lane road wasn't deserted by any means. She did need to watch for the sharp curves.

She reached over and took his hand. "Don't worry, Barry. Whoever this shooter is, we'll get him. Now that we know he's after us, we'll be careful to stay hidden. The hotel we can stay at isn't far from the fellowship's office. Milkan is a great guy, and he'll rally the troops to help us catch this person."

He noticed her glance at her rearview mirror again, her brows drawing down. He twisted in his seat and looked out the back window. "What's wrong?"

"Probably nothing. I'm just paranoid now. But the same car has been behind us for a while."

"Maybe they're going into town, too."

"That's it, I'm sure. There are only a couple of ways into town." She slowed to make the curve. The car didn't slow; it seemed to speed up.

Barry spun in his seat. "Brace yourself. They're going to ram—" Their bodies whipped forward and snapped back. Charli barely kept the SUV on the road. The tires screeched as she overcorrected off the soft shoulder into oncoming traffic. The deep blast of a semitruck directly in front of them filled their ears.

The car that had rammed them blocked Charli from getting back into the right lane. Barry clutched the door's armrest and the center console. He could only pray he'd see his beloved Charli in whatever came after death. He glanced at the car's driver, the maniac trying to kill them. The man's eyes looked straight ahead, unblinking.

Barry felt his body jerk sideways and his forehead hit the passenger window, then he saw the side of the semi zip past him. He was still breathing and the SUV was still moving. He glanced at Charli, white-knuckled hands gripping the wheel. She was fantastic.

She swerved the SUV back into their lane, now behind the car. "You fucking asshole!" she yelled at the windshield. "I just made the last payment on this truck, and *now* it's dented. Not by a crazy cow or fucking farm animal, but a lunatic trying to kill us. Dammit."

Barry was sure she'd lost touch with reality with that rant. The attacker's car in front didn't pull away. He said, "I don't know what he can do being ahead of us, but be ready."

She slowed the truck and glanced in the rearview. "Shit, someone's behind us and my taillights are probably busted. We gotta get off this road." She continued to slow and the car behind passed them on a solid yellow line. The muscle car sped by both cars on the narrowed stretch and disappeared around the next corner.

The crazy-ass driver in front of them slowed in relation to their speed, never far from the front of the SUV. Barry didn't know the road, but looked at the ravine over the side. This was not the place to pull over. And if they did stop, then what? His bear wanted blood. Someone was trying to hurt his mate, but Barry knew they wanted him. Something inside told him he was the one bringing the heat.

Suddenly, the SUV kicked into a lower gear and jumped forward. His hands regripped his holding spots. "Charli, baby, what are you doing?"

For fuck's sake, she was going to get herself killed. She wasn't like him. They both knew he could heal faster than her. If she got hurt . . . His bear roared at the mere thought. His control on the animal slipped. He had to fight to stay in human form.

"If the damn Mustang can do it, so can I." The truck swung into the other lane and burst forward. "Watch this." At the slow speed the car was going, the truck zipped by it. But the car started catching up quickly. Charli had to slow to make the curve. The guy kept coming. If she could swing them around without going over the side, they'd be okay and the car would crash. At its rate of speed, there was no way physics wouldn't allow for it.

They were almost clear when the car tagged the rear bumper, fish-tailing the truck. This time, the lane was too narrow for the sharp hit and both SUV and car careened over the side.

CHAPTER TWENTY-NINE

B arry jerked awake and regretted the sudden movement. A burning pain zinged from his neck to his foot. His eyes opened and the past sixty seconds flooded his head. He hung sideways in his seat, the belt holding him tightly as the SUV lay on its driver's side.

He reached toward his love lying on the door, blood staining the cracked glass. *No, no, no, no!* Not her.

"Charli. Sweetheart?" He wrapped his hand around her bicep and felt the pulse in her arm. She was alive. Relief released the band around his chest and he took in a deep breath. Someone was getting killed. Even if he could stop himself from attacking, the bear was too far gone with anger. His mate was hurt. He wasn't letting that shit go.

He struggled to stay calm. He couldn't help her if he didn't think straight. His bear's thoughts fought his own. The animal wanted blood. Revenge. He wanted someone hurting for the fact that Charli was passed out and bleeding. It dawned on him how attached his bear was to her. Not only was Barry himself feeling a lot more than he expected for her as a man, but the bear, he treasured her. Charli was the animal's life.

My mate. My reason for being.

He finally understood some of the unusual dominant thoughts and actions he struggled with. This bear had claimed Charli as his own, and while he would happily share her with Barry, he wouldn't allow anyone to hurt her. Barry wouldn't either. Except at that moment, getting her some help and ensuring her wellbeing was more important than going after their attacker.

Stay calm and figure out the best plan of attack. He realized there was no way he could get Charli out with the truck on its side. If he could manage to gently tip it onto four wheels, then he could easily get to her. He fumbled for the seatbelt release, pushed the red center, but nothing happened. The release mechanism was jammed. *Fuck.*

He needed a knife or scissors to cut the material. He was so screwed. He took another breath and smelled no gasoline, so, hopefully, that meant an explosion wasn't imminent. What else could he cut the belt with? He felt the other presence in his head. A dull pain shot through his finger. He looked down to see a vicious-looking claw where his fingernail used to be.

"Fuck, that's cool. Handy, too." His new talon sliced through the thick fabric, and he watched as it retracted into his finger and the nail regrew. Good as new. "I really need to learn this shifter shit." Using his additional strength, he busted the window with his elbow and crawled out. He hit the ground, his knees buckling, to land on the grass.

He groaned and rolled his head to see the undercarriage of the tipped SUV. A small shiny rectangle attached near the wheelbase caught his eye. He rolled forward and pried it from the metal. He didn't know how he knew, but he recognized this as a tracking device.

A loud roar emanated from his chest. The bear got more pissed by the minute.

"Son of a bitch. We were sitting ducks. Who the fuck is this bastard?" He tilted his head back, an even louder roar ripping from his chest. Frustration added to his emotional and physical state. He didn't know who it was or why they were after them, but he knew one thing for sure: they weren't going to hurt his woman again. He'd give up his life before he allowed that to happen. Charli's life was priceless.

The grinding of metal against metal several yards away drew his attention. The car trying to run them off the road lay upside down. The driver's side door pushed open and the man he'd seen driving fell out. Damn, he looked beat to shit and back. He'd deal with him later. After he got Charli out.

Zombie eyes met his and the man opened his mouth. Wider and wider. His teeth sharpened to points, and nose and jaw punched out into a muzzle. Brown fur exploded from his scalp and grew out like a domino effect down his body. His clothes busted at the seams and fell to the ground in scraps. Had Barry blinked, he would have missed the entire morphing of man to animal. It was surreal.

Within a few seconds, Barry watched the male morph into a bear. If he hadn't seen it with his own eyes, he never would've believed it. "Holy fuck." Then he realized, he was the same thing. Shit, two could tango.

He stepped away from the SUV, pulling up his sleeves. If the bastard wanted a fight, that's what he'd get. "Come on, you furry piece of shit. Let's rumble." The bear reared up on his hind legs and roared. Damn, that was pretty impressive. He couldn't wait to do his own.

And he waited. He lifted his human hands. No claws or fur.

The other bear came down to all fours.

Barry rubbed his hands over his face. No razor teeth or snout.

The monster stalked toward him.

He examined his clothes. No tearing. Shit, they were still a little baggy.

The beast charged and Barry ran for the woods. Shit, shit, shit. This was not good. *Hey, up there*, he said in his head. *I could use a little help here.* He felt the other presence, but it was unattached, as if watching from the sideline and laughing. *Let me remind you, animal, if I die, so do you.* His bear's ears perked up. Chrissakes, did he have the slowest bear in the shed? His animal growled. Great. Now he pissed it off. He was fucked.

Barry looked over his shoulder to see the other beast having a hard time maneuvering around the trees and brush. Score one point for two feet. He slowed to get his bearings. He didn't want to get too far from the SUV and Charli. Cutting to the side, he worked back the way he'd come. Well, he thought he did.

After a few minutes, nothing looked familiar. Not that he could distinguish one tree from the other, anyway. His previous life was probably not Grizzly Adams-ish. Well, except for the bear part, obviously.

Worrying less about the roaming monster, he hurried his step. How far was he from the wreck site? And where was the other bear? He didn't smell anything nearby. Grunt sounds came from not too far away. The screech of bending metal rented the air. The SUV. The killer was after Charli.

Powered by his now-mindful other half, he flew past trunks and leaped piles of stickers and brush. He didn't know where he was going. He put full trust into his partner's paws to guide him to Charli.

He shot out from the tree line to see the beast bust the driver's side window on the righted SUV. Barry opened his mouth to yell, but instead a roar louder than before ripped from him. The other beast stepped back from the door and answered with his own growl. Barry dove at the bear, wondering what in the fuck he was doing. He was insane, trying to take down a massive animal as a human.

Then he saw his hands—make that paws—stretch for the enemy's throat. He'd be damned. He *was* a shifter. How had that happened? While he pondered his new body, his bear fought for their mate. He knew how his bear felt when it was tucked inside as he was now. Weird. He was there for the show, but wasn't a part of it. Should he be?

Barry tried to exert some control over his bear. He felt the animal falter, then pain ripped through his chest as the other beast raked claws across his fur. Before he could do anything else, he was on his back, staring into black, soulless eyes. He rolled his head slightly to the side so the drop of spit hanging on a stretched thread from the other's mouth wouldn't fall into his. That was enough to make him puke.

Since he moved his own head, he worried that maybe his bear had relinquished motor control. They weren't exactly kicking ass like they were a second ago. Shit. What did he have to do to get his bear back?

The beast on top of him reared back, arm and claws extended, ready to make the death blow. Barry wanted to fight, but something inside made him shrink away. He hated that feeling. He knew he was no coward. What was holding him back? He squeezed his eyes shut.

Charli's body hurt everywhere. She wasn't sure where she was or why she was slumped over. Slowly, she sat back, swallowing the bile that rose from her stomach. Her head thumped with the pressure of a squished balloon.

Growls and grunts came from outside the SUV. Though her vision was blurry, she could make out two massive bears a few yards behind the vehicle. Then her mind kicked in and she remembered the car pushing them off the road.

Barry's door was open. Then she realized he had to be one of the bears. They were circling each other, but not fighting at the moment. She pulled her phone from her back pocket and tried to focus on the buttons. Her vision was doubled. She wanted 911, but she got only one of her speed dial numbers pushed before the device slipped from her fingers.

She heard her boss's voice on the line. "Milkan," she said. "Wreck. Interstate south, town. Help." Out her window, roars erupted between the fighting bears. One of the bears was overpowering the other, almost ready to finish the weaker one off.

Adrenaline electrified her brain and limbs. Instinctively, she knew Barry was the bear on the bottom, the one about to die. She fumbled through the center console and pulled out her Glock. With the longer distance, her vision was better. She forced her door open, stumbled against a tree to steady her aim, and fired until the top bear retreated.

Once Barry was safe, the gun fell from her hand and she felt herself slip to the ground.

CHAPTER THIRTY

Devin stuck the pushpin through the top of the photo, attaching it to the corkboard section of the wall. The path from the bank's employee door to the vault room was clearly marked. At the corner sat the break room. He put up a blank piece of paper to show where the hall ran past the supply room to the door leading to the alley and dumpster.

Russel came in with a smile on his face. Either the man was perpetually happy, or finding his mate made him that way.

Devin wouldn't know that feeling. He'd waited years and traveled everywhere he could to look for her. His cat wanted a family to love and a mate to snuggle with. His heart wanted the same. To keep sane, he buried himself in work like many other workaholics. His mother, God rest her soul, always told him to be patient. Fate would guide him to her. Have faith.

Not too long ago, his faith in everything had been shattered. Transferring here literally saved his life.

He sighed. He didn't want to go there. He'd been in a bad place at that time, but managed to crawl out of that hole thanks in part to his new environment. Now he wanted to do everything he could to protect those who gave him his second chance. The answer was so close . . .

Russel tossed another paper ball at him. "Hey, cat. You look like you're going to have a coronary. Come out to happy hour with me now and get a couple of beers. We'll work through your case."

He was about to do his usual and turn down anything that took his mind off work and onto his life, but Russel wasn't done talking.

"And if you tell me no, I swear to God, I'll drag all my sisters and their friends and the cousins in here with fifteen pizzas and let them tell you about their sex lives all night."

He laughed and raised his hands in defeat. "All right, Mayer. You're buying the first round."

"Woo-hoo. You got it. Let's go." Russel clapped him on the back. "It's nice to have a beer buddy again. But unfortunately, I found my mate, so you're gonna have to find another buddy."

Devin frowned. "Shouldn't you be with her?"

"Yeah," Russel began, "but not until my place is spotless. The neighbor kids are gonna clean it for two hundred bucks tomorrow. They talk a tough game. They even have a power washer for the downstairs bathroom."

"Is that the one you don't sit on?"

Russel let out a loud guffaw. "Man, you got the memory of a sperm whale."

Sperm whale? Devin wasn't sure how to take that. Knowing the few things that seemed to overwhelmingly occupy Russel's mind—sex and more sex—he wondered if the whole joke was on *sperm*. "Why a sperm whale and not an elephant?"

"The whale has the biggest brain at seventeen pounds. So, larger brain . . . larger capacity . . . can remember more. Get it?"

Devin wanted to laugh at the insane comparison, but he'd keep the funny to himself.

Russel slapped his back again as they walked out the department's door, heading for the bar down the street. "I can see where you thought an elephant might work. The elephant has the biggest dick of any land animal. Six feet long. Can you imagine?" No. He didn't want to imagine. Russel raised a hand over his head. "That's as tall as I am."

Oh shit. His new friend walked right into this. "So if someone called you a total dick, they'd be right?"

Russel stopped and bent over laughing. "Shit, man. That was great." He held his stomach from laughing so hard. "But if that ever gets out, I'm siccing my unmarried cousin on you. She's cute, but has a vicious bite."

Reaching the entrance, Russel held the door for Devin, and they both entered the dim area with loud music. They each took a stool at the bar and ordered brews. After a long swallow, Russel sat back. "Okay, man. What's got your brain in a noodle? Spell out the clues and let ol' Russ here show you the light."

Going back and forth, the two listed possible connections, brainstormed reasons the woman would be naked—according to Russel, she probably belonged to the nudist colony that went to the beach every summer. Not that he was part of the group. He was banned after he somehow got a fish to bite the head honcho's dick in the lake. It required stitches. The nurses laughed for days after treating the guy.

"Let's find a quieter table," Devin said. Russel ordered two more beers and guided them to an empty table in the back corner.

"Whatcha thinking?" Russel asked.

"I remember in the manager's office at the jewelry store, she had blankets on the floor that looked like a small animal slept on them. And you joked that you smelled cat."

Russel held up a finger. "If I remember correctly, I said pussy."

"Yeah, but you meant cat." Devin paused and thought about it. "You didn't mean cat, did you?" Russel slapped the table and laughed. Even Devin couldn't deny the humor.

"Actually, I did mean cat." His face turned serious. "Most of you cats smell pretty much the same. But there are subtleties among you that make each feline have his own smell. And when I think back to both locations and the smells, the cat in each is the same cat."

Devin slapped his forehead and leaned back. "You know what that means?"

Russel thought a moment, then said, "There's a cat with really bad luck walking around?"

Before Devin could answer, his phone rang. "Sonder here." Milkan's voice came on, loudly telling him Charli was in the hospital from a wreck. "We'll check on her. Leaving now."

CHAPTER
THIRTY-ONE

A stabbing pain woke Charli. Her eyelids were too heavy to open and since it hurt her head to breathe, she wasn't keen on seeing anything. Rhythmic beeps kept time with the pulse in her throat. It sounded like she was in her clinic's minor operating room. But she didn't remember taking in any injuries. The pregnant cow was the last patient she remembered seeing.

The wreck flashed through her mind. Oh shit. An image of fighting bears and the concussion of gunshots floated in her head. Were they part of a dream or real?

Where was Barry? Where was she, for that matter? Forcing one eye open, she worried the light in the room would make her head ache worse. But the dimness was soft enough for her to open her other lid.

Barry sat twisted in an upholstered chair scooted against the hospital bed, his hand holding hers, asleep. He would have a neck cramp certainly. He looked adorable in light-blue scrubs, his hair sticking up in different directions. His scruffy chin made him even hotter.

His nose twitched and his eyes popped open. They were dark, saturated with desire. His grin was quick. "Someone is having naughty thoughts in this room, and it's not just me."

She choked out a laugh, causing her skull and ribs to burn. "Shit, Barry. Don't make me laugh. I'll kick your ass, I hurt so much."

He stood from his chair, then leaned over and gently took her lips with his. That didn't help to douse the heat in her or slow the blood pumping through her head. Only one thing pumping in her would relieve the hot desire.

"Whatever you're thinking," Barry began between kisses, "you'd better stop or we're about to start playing doctor right here in front of all the nurses. Fuck, you smell incredible."

A woman in green scrubs and a light cotton jacket with cute mice all over it walked in. "Yup, what we thought, missy. Your heart rate was up quite a bit, so we figured this fine specimen of man in here was attacking you. Let me take your vitals, then the attack can resume." The nurse winked at her and she felt her cheeks flood hot.

Barry stepped back, a grin from ear to ear making his eyes sparkle. After the attendant left, he grabbed up Charli's hand and kissed each knuckle. "I can't tell you how close to panicked I was. You wouldn't open your eyes and barely breathed. I thought I was going to lose you."

"Aw, Barry. You say the sweetest things. I'm damn hard to get rid of. Especially when you have me wrapped around your finger."

"Right," Barry grunted. "It's me around your finger"—he kissed her wrist—"and your body"—he sucked on the inside of her elbow, releasing it with a pop—"and in your body. Coming hard enough to make your legs tremble for hours."

A chill ran through her whole body. That sounded so heavenly. "But first, my love, you have to heal enough for us to go home."

Shit. He was right. "What about the shooter, though?"

He plopped back into his chair next to the bed. "I think I know how the killer was keeping tabs on us. After the truck crashed, I found a tracking device attached to the undercarriage."

Her eyes opened wide. "Tracking device?"

He nodded with a mean-looking frown. "Seems our friend wants to be more than a mere acquaintance."

"Dammit, now what?" She bit her lip and wondered what they could do next.

"Hey, no worrying. I'm in charge here and will take care of it all. You just need to tell me what to do." He smiled and met her gaze. "Let's figure it out together."

The scene of the accident played in her mind. Then she remembered the bears. "Barry, you shifted, didn't you? How'd you manage that?"

He turned contemplative, his finger rubbing over his chin. He was so cute when serious. "I don't know. I told myself it was time to shift when the bear was coming for me, but it didn't work. I shifted when I saw the other bear at your driver's window, busting it open to go after you. Then it happened so quickly, I didn't even know until I saw my hands were paws."

"Ah," Charli said. "I remember something about my shifter training saying mates will fight to the death for the other. That usually happens in the animal form because it's usually the stronger one. When you saw I was in danger, your bear came out without asking or telling."

His grin started with love in his eyes and ended with a wicked slyness. "Does that mean what I think it means? Mate?"

Mate? She should deny it, but that wasn't going to be true, and he'd know she was lying. Plus, she wasn't going to start lying now. Barry had opened up doors in her heart she'd long thought closed. She'd fallen quickly for his openness and his protectiveness. People didn't protect her. She was on her own. But now there was Barry, and maybe she didn't have to be alone anymore. Should she tell him that? Probably not.

She rolled her eyes and coughed out a giggle. "First, tell me what happened after I shot the bear. It was a shifter, not a real bear, right? Where did he come from?"

"It was a shifter." Barry rubbed her hand in circles, thinking. She glanced at the way he continued to go back and forth with his thumb over her palm, the motion soothing and erotic at the same time. "It was the guy trying to run us off the road. And if I'm correct, he wore the same zombie face you said I wore when I was unloading the money bags, which are still missing."

Charli met his eyes. "Something's going on here. Something bigger than just you and me. Go on. Did Milkan get there? I called him."

"Yeah. He said he would take care of everything at the scene. I needed to take care of you. He got there not long after you saved my tail." He twisted to look down his backside. "Bears have tails, don't they?"

Charli smiled. He'd done the silliness purposely to make her smile. "Yes, they have cute little ones. Turn around and let me see yours." He spun around and wiggled his tight ass for her. She itched to get her hands on it as he drilled into her. A surge of desire shot through her. Barry turned and part groaned, part growled.

"Woman, you will be my undoing." He swooped down, running his lips down her neck, breathing deeply. His hand skimmed the side of her breast, thumb rubbing the hardening nubbin.

She ran her fingers through his hair. "When can I leave?" She paused. "Better yet, does the door lock?"

Barry chuckled and put his forehead against hers. "Doctor said you should be fine, and he'll decide if you can go when he does his rounds in the morning. I am so relieved you're safe. I was afraid of losing you. When we get out of here, I'm hiding you away for a year and never letting anyone touch you but me."

"A year? What about my clinic?" she teased.

"You can talk to the animals on the phone, and we'll hire an assistant to administer meds there."

She almost laughed. "I can't talk to them on the phone, silly. I need physical contact with them. You know that."

"Well, they'd better learn ESP fast because your hands belong to me." He scooped them into his and kissed the scratched skin.

She pouted as if in thought. "I'll think about it. Even though you fight like a wuss."

His face went from happy tears to a playful frown. "It was my first shift that I remember. We were figuring things out."

She snorted. "Yeah, well, Tom can fight better than you right now."

"The squirrel? I'll take him on any day. Wait. Is he a shifter, too?"

Charli started a laugh and regretted it. Barry saw her pained expression and winced. "Sorry, sweetheart. Doc said you have bruised ribs, but nothing is broken. You have a bump on your head they want to watch. Could be a minor concussion. But hopefully not." That explained her thumping head. She needed several hydrocodone before she was bouncing on her toes like Marika.

Charli wondered if the shooter knew about their trip to FAWS. She prayed he didn't. Who would protect Marika?

CHAPTER THIRTY-TWO

Devin pushed on the hospital door to room 610. Charli's smile greeted him. The deadweight pressing on him lifted when he saw she was alive and looked fine. He hadn't realized how quickly he'd taken his two coworkers into his heart as family. That's what they were now. An invisible bond had snuck up on him and tied his ass to a multimorph and an animal whisperer. Well, there were worse things to be attached to.

He approached Charli on the opposite side of the hospital bed from where Barry sat. Devin brushed back the hair from her face and planted a kiss on her forehead. A low growl vibrated in the air from Barry. "Chill, bear. This is my little sister now. And I will treat her as such."

Charli raised her brows. "You might want to talk to my siblings before you volunteer for that position. I was known to play some pretty nasty tricks on them growing up."

"So was I." He winked at her. "How are you feeling?"

"As good as can be expected when someone runs you off the road and down a cliff."

"Tell us what happened, Charli," Russel said as he entered the room and leaned against the wall.

She looked at Barry, then to them. "So much has happened in almost two days. And not all of it good. But we need to compare notes since Barry and I have information that might help you with the robberies."

Devin was a bit taken aback. How could she have something that tied to his cases? Had she been holding out evidence? He felt suspicion creep into his mind.

Charli rolled her eyes and smiled. "No, Devin. I haven't withheld any evidence that would be helpful at any point to you."

His eyes popped wide. "I thought you could only read animals' minds. How did you—"

"Relax," Charli said with a grin. "I'm not reading your mind. You're a male, and an investigator at that. I knew what you were thinking by looking at you."

A flash of terror passed over Russel's face. "Can all women do that? I am so fucked." Laughter released the tension that had grown since the men walked in.

"Russel, you are so much more than fucked from what I've seen of Detective Gibbons," Charli said.

Russel crossed his arms over his chest. "Yeah, that's what Milkan keeps sayin'. Y'all just wait and see. You haven't seen me in action yet."

"Thank god for small miracles," Devin added. "Now what about this evidence you're withholding?" He grinned and winked again.

She went through the happenings of the past day and a half, from finding Barry to being run off the road. Then Devin and Russel shared their facts. When finished, Devin flipped through the pages of notes he'd taken.

"Okay, where does that leave us? What do we know about the female robber?"

"She has long hair, walks around naked, never enters or leaves by conventional means," Charli said.

"She's a missing person from DC, according to those other investigators," Barry added.

"How did she get all the way across the country, and why open a cleaning business when she got here?" Charli asked. "If she was hiding, seems to me she'd go incognito instead of robbing places. And naked, of all things."

"Why would she be naked?" Devin asked, quickly amending, "Disregarding being a nudist, Russel."

They had to ponder that. "She likes to show off her junk. Air it out from time to time." Russel was so tactful with his words.

"Try again." Devin scowled. "And don't worry about being politically correct or anything, Mayer."

He looked out the window overlooking the parking lot. "Maybe she . . . didn't want clothing constricting her any, or catching on something."

"No," Charli gasped. "She's naked from just shifting. Like Barry always is." Realizing what she had said and the audience, her face blossomed with red cheeks.

Russel laughed. "No problems there, Charli. Shifters are used to that kind of thing. Walking around naked is second nature to us."

Barry and Devin turned to Russel.

"Not all of us," they both said.

Russel snorted. "Y'all are prudes. Get over yourselves." He spread his arms wide and shook his hips side to side. "Embrace the freedom. Let your junk live as nature intended."

Charli threw a pillow at him. "Mayer, you so much as moon me and I'll have your mate on your ass in no time."

A big grin spread over Russel's face. "I like that idea. Both of you come to my place tomorrow. The toilet will be cleaned first thing." The couple looked at each other, then to Devin.

"Don't ask." Devin flipped to a new page. "All right. Our thief is a shifter. What kind? Does it matter?"

"Well, yeah," Charli said. "If she's small enough, she could crawl through holes and under doors, right? Not setting off the alarms."

"Holy shit." Barry sat back in his chair. "Are there roach shifters? That'd be really weird."

Devin thought about that idea. Maybe not an insect, since he'd never heard of any animals but mammals, for the most part. What about a mouse? They were small. The image of the cat walking down the bank hall in the security footage came to mind. Mice probably wouldn't get far with a cat on duty. Then it clicked for him.

"She's a cat."

Russel snapped his head around. A grin formed on his face. "You are freakin'-A right, brother. Both places smelled of the same cat."

"As did the cleaning lady's place," Devin said.

Russel popped away from the wall, approaching the bed. "Remember what the homeless guy said about the cleaning lady having snake eyes? Which resemble cat eyes, at times."

Then their faces expressed *halleluiah*. "The cleaning lady is the thief!"

They remained quiet for a moment, letting the new info soak in. Devin leaned over and kissed Charli's forehead again. "Okay, Charli. You two stay here and get better. Keep hidden so the shooter doesn't know where you are. I promise we'll get him, Charli." He spun away and snagged Russel's arm. "Sinatra and I have something to do."

The two men walked out the door. Devin was on a mission, and he was finishing it tonight.

CHAPTER
THIRTY-THREE

Russel sat in the passenger's seat as Devin pushed through traffic. Well, what consisted of traffic in Shedford—a backup at the
stoplight.

"I'm missing something," Russel said. "You know something I don't
because the connection isn't clear-cut to me."

"That's very possible. If I'm wrong, I'd rather you stop me before I
make a total ass of myself."

"Better that than a complete dick, my friend."

Devin laughed and slapped the steering wheel. "You are so fucked
up, Sinatra. You definitely keep me on my toes."

"Ain't nobody accused me of being sane. I have a reputation to
uphold in the shifter community."

"That's good," Devin said. "Now, strip."

Russel sat back, hand over his chest. "Who told you I was a stripper? I'll kill her for tattling."

Devin glanced at him. "You're a stripper? Women pay to see *you* naked?"

"Hey, we're not a fabric-free establishment, I'm proud to say. And yes, in my world, I can make this flesh look more than perfect. It's only the weekend, anyway." He looked at Devin. "And why do you want me to strip? Did you grow up surrounded by females? Hmmm."

Devin snorted. "Not quite, chicken legs. You need to strip because you're going in."

He blinked. "In where?"

"To get some pussy." Devin's grin reminded him of the Cheshire cat from hell.

Russel groaned. "Oh man. You tell me that *now*, after I've found my mate? You have lousy timing."

"Actually, the timing is perfect. I'm betting on two-week intervals."

"For what?"

"The bank heist was four weeks ago. The jewelry store was two weeks."

"Ah, so you're thinking she will strike any day." So far, Russel felt good about his fellow agent's conclusion. "Where? Besides money and jewelry, there's not much more to steal."

"That's the genius of her plan. By stealing things, the police are watching all the stores and places with money. What was her job in DC?"

"Her background is working with a water company."

"Perfect. Now when we passed that building today, what did we see?"

Russel let out a whistle. "We saw the fluffy black cat in the bank video crossing the street to the utility building." He shook his head, amazed. They finally made it through the light to see a fender bender blocking two lanes, making the bad intersection worse.

"You got it. I'm betting in the last two weeks, she's bamboozled her way into an employee's office. When we almost hit the cat crossing the street, she was on her way there to be let in to hide before everyone left for the weekend."

Russel jumped in. "No alarms needed because she was already inside. Then the next day, when the first person opens the office—"

"She leaves with no one being the wiser."

"Damn, that's brilliant." He shook his head. "But wait. Why the utility company?"

"Yeah, haven't gotten that far in figuring this out."

"Okay, now what? You want me to go in to see if she's there? Then call the police?"

"If she's a shifter, then we need to take care of it. Or at least give Chief Charter time to gather the right team."

Russel unbuttoned his shirt. "Either way is fine. Let me find out if she's there and what she's up to." They passed the building and parked in a neighboring lot around back.

Devin asked, "What are you going in as?"

Russel pulled his socks and shoes off as Devin headed to the trunk of the car. "I'm thinking a badass Mickey Mouse would be good. Small enough to get through any crack in the exterior and walk around on the ceiling tiles." The parking lot they sat in had broken and crumbled asphalt, but it was trash free. No beer bottles, candy wrappers, or soft drink cans. Just muddy from the last rain.

"Hey," Russel called from the front seat, "why do I get to do the dirty stuff?"

"Didn't one of your own call you 'dirty rats'?" Devin snickered behind the car.

He unbuttoned his pants. "Look, man, if you're gonna quote the classics, you gotta get them right. Everyone knows Cagney said 'dirty, double-crossin' rat.' How about some rat jokes?"

"How about not," came Devin's reply.

"Where does a rat get a new tail?" Russel paused. When he didn't get an answer, he continued. "A re-tail store. What did one lab rat say to another?" This time he didn't wait. "I have my scientist trained so well that every time I push my button, he brings me a treat. Okay, last one. How many rats does it take to unscrew a lightbulb? None. They already chewed through the wire and that's why the bulb's out in the first place." He shifted, becoming small.

Laughter rang from the side of the car. "Haven't heard that one." Devin opened the driver's door and slid inside. He opened the small box he'd retrieved from the trunk and took out a tiny camera attached to a little collar. "All right, Sinatra. Sit on the center console here, and I'll strap the camera on."

A spew of squeaks and sounds came from him sitting on the passenger seat. Damn, he'd forgotten he shifted. He was not wearing a stupid camera. He didn't give a rat's ass what his coworker wanted.

"What? We have the thing, why not use it? Besides, I haven't gotten to play with it yet. You're a great guinea pig. I mean, rat." Devin's smile widened. Russel Rat sat up on his hind legs and crossed his little arms. "Okay, sorry. Relax."

Devin fumbled more with the camera. "Come on, don't act like a spoiled rat. I want to see what you see. We might need it for evidence."

He had a point. Video evidence was rather compelling. But one more lame rat comment, after not laughing at any of his, and he'd jump in Devin's lap and bite his balls.

He hopped onto the console between the seats and held his tiny arms up. Devin wrapped the Velcro collar around his little chest. When Devin hit his ticklish spot, he wiggled and squeaked.

"Oh, aren't you so cute. I bet your mate will love finding that spot."

Another burst of squeaks came from his mouth, irritating him. Shifters didn't talk about others' mates. Damn cat. If only he could transform his vocal cords, all would be well. Instead, he swiped at Devin's hand and pointed a little finger/toe at him in warning.

Devin laughed. "Okay, little man. I got it." Devin configured the camera so the front rested just above his head. Then he pulled out a cell phone-sized monitor and clicked the power button. Instantly, the inside of Devin's car appeared on the screen. "That looks good. Too bad we don't have a way to communicate. We'll have to create something and call them Mickey ears."

Russel gave a low grunt to show his displeasure. The cat did not understand rat humor.

"Do you want me to carry you to the building or you want to go on your own?"

He wondered why his co-agent kept asking him questions. Like Devin was going to understand rat language. He crawled to the passenger door, pushed the unlock button, and looked over his shoulder at Devin.

"I'll take that as you'll get there on your own." Devin leaned over and opened the door, then Russel was gone.

CHAPTER
THIRTY-FOUR

Russel scampered across the abandoned parking lot toward the brick waterworks building. There was about an hour before twilight, and he wanted to get this over with so he could get started building a nest for his mate. Since Devin was OCD with neatness, maybe he should ask Devin to organize his place so his rat's nest wouldn't look like . . . wait for it . . . a rat's nest. He laughed to himself.

Something big caught his eye as he hurried across the street. He felt something jar his side and slide under the belt holding the camera. He went around and around and around until he realized what had happened. He grabbed onto the bristles caught under the camera collar, jerked them out, then waited for the right time to release his hold.

He flew through the air, ejected from the street cleaner that had sucked him up. Whoa, he needed to be careful when thinking of his mate. She took over his complete consciousness. That happened to his uncle Rupert. Tragic story.

His uncle had just met his mate at the annual shifter rally, and on their first date, he took her to the local arena hockey game. Like most males, he was trying to impress his woman with his manly shifter abilities. So when the rink cleared for a game break, he shifted into his mate's favorite animal, a cute pink-eared bunny rabbit, and scrambled onto the ice, ohhing and ahhing the crowd with his four-footed skating skills.

He was only thinking of his beautiful mate while twisting and turning, then—bam! He was sucked into the Zamboni machine. It wasn't pretty. Russel's mom, Rupert's sister, never went to another hockey game again. Sad.

He scuttled along the base of the brick building, looking for an entrance. Ah, crumbled debris lay beneath a pipe going into the wall. He loved old buildings. The camera made the entrance a bit tighter, but he wiggled through and found his way into the ceiling for easier access across the rooms.

The smell of cat was fresh and strong. The cleaning cat lady had to be here. Now, where in the ten thousand square feet was she? He followed his nose to the highest concentration of kitty. He chewed through the fibrous ceiling tile and stuck his nose through it. Yup, bigtime pussy cat.

He pulled his nose up and put an eyeball to the hole. Looked like a regular office. He spotted a pile of blankets in the corner behind the desk. The perp's hideaway for the past two weeks. Nice. Even had toys that looked pretty cool. He smelled treats. Maybe there was a stash hidden in the desk. They smelled *really* good. He hadn't eaten since lunch six hours ago.

A closing door snapped him out of his food daze. He was on a mission and had to get this job done so he could focus on his mate again. Damn cat. Scrabbling across rusty pipes and frayed wires, he headed toward the freshest line of scent.

The newer smells led him to a ceiling tile with a hole already torn in it. His head fit through with the camera. She sat at a computer in a big room with lots of office machines and desks. Russel watched her type and stare at the monitor. He couldn't see the screen from his angle; he'd have to get lower.

He wrapped his tail around a pipe and slowly inched out of the hole. The scene in *Mission Impossible* where Cruise comes through the ceiling on a rope came to mind. He spread his tiny arms, bouncing his ass end to the movie's theme song playing in his head.

When he lowered enough, the screen came into view. It looked like she was entering data for a customer. Why in the hell would she be doing that? It made no sense.

The sound of water rushing through pipes caught his ear, but he thought nothing of it until the pipe his tail was wrapped around began to heat. And heat it did. Within a couple of seconds, his body screamed from the burning pain. He hated old buildings. He released his tail and fell smack onto the keyboard the lady typed on.

Her zombie eyes stared straight ahead, but her fingers stopped moving under him. Instincts had him ready to run, but she didn't move, so neither did he. He sat up on his back legs and waved his arms in her line of sight. Nothing. She barely blinked.

He stretched his foot to the side to touch her hand. With contact, he jerked back like touching a hot stove. Again nothing. Slowly, he extended his foot again and laid it on her hand. With no movement from her, he dragged the rest of his body onto her hand. This chick was really out of it. Was she on drugs?

His feet moved back and forth in a cha-cha up her arm. Sinatra really was a perfect name for him, but he'd never say that out loud. On a cha, his foot slipped off the side of her arm, leaving a bleeding scratch. The woman startled. He froze. Her head snapped toward him, eyes turning to green with slits.

Oh shit. His rat's ass was toast.

She hissed and swung at him with claws on her other hand. He dove for his life, scrawny arms and legs stretched out to catch air to slow his crash landing. Didn't really matter. It wasn't like he was falling from plane height. But he bet he looked cool. If only his mate could've seen it.

He landed with a smack and scrambled for traction on the shiny tile. A large shadow cast on him. He turned to see a fluffy black cat flying toward him. Claws extended on four feet, mouth open with sharp teeth ready to chomp. This was one time he didn't want pussy on his face.

He took off, running under desks and around chairs, trying to lose his assassin. She was good. The rat race was on.

Russel kept his cool, knowing panic would rat out his logic. Then he'd be stuck like a rat in a cage. In the darkened room ahead, light sliced along the floor. The door to the hall was open. Maybe he could escape like rats abandoning a sinking ship.

Along the straight path to the door, he lined up with the narrow slit, ready to hit it on a dead run like a rat being chased by a cat. Which he was. With millimeters to spare, Russel slipped through. He wondered how wide the cat's head was when he heard a thunk and an angry meow. Definitely a pissed pussy.

He glanced over his nonexistent shoulder to see the kitty pushing the door wider, then zeroing in on him. Dinner. Rats, he shouldn't have stopped to look. Spinning out on the slick floor, he took off down the hall, searching for a way out of the crazy maze he was stuck in.

He rounded a corner and his front end turned, but his heavier back end slid to the side, slapping into a janitor's yellow mop bucket. He winced with the contact. That would hurt in the morning. He was tender under his smooth, flawless skin.

The lady janitor looked up as he scrambled away. She squealed like a stuck rat and jumped around as if Russel was attacking her. Oh please, he thought, he wasn't rat-shit crazy. He was getting the hell out of Dodge. He didn't have time to play cat and mouse with her.

Before he got far, the big kitty came around the corner. Her claws did not stop her slide toward the bucket either. She slammed into the side, scaring the shit out of the janitor again. Dirty water sloshed over, dousing the animal, making the pussy look like a drowned rat.

The lady with the ratty mop stabbed at them both, trying to get away from two creatures who didn't give a rat's ass about her.

He whipped around another corner, and salvation sat on the other side. He loved old buildings. Sprinting like his tail was on fire, he prepared for his grand exit. But kitty was gaining ground with her longer strides. Three feet from the end of the hall, Russel launched himself into the air. The camera made him heavier than normal, so he had to adjust on the fly.

He lined up with the words Mail Slot four feet off the floor and pointed his toes for a perfect ten-point-oh dive into the chute. Behind him, he heard a splat against the outer wall and a roar of a meow. He chuckled. He'd never been in a rat race that he'd lost. And he wasn't about to change it.

During his descent, his butt once again took the lead. He hoped his mate liked big butts. And he could not lie, he liked a lot of flesh to sink his teeth into. His little body was getting hot thinking about his mate. Mmm. He did love a woman in uniform.

A faint light shone below, getting closer and closer. The chute curved up at the last second and shot him through the air, over the mail cart, to crash into a stack of empty taped-up shipping boxes. Cardboard pummeled him as he tried to protect his head with arms that didn't quite do the trick. He was able to cover his ears and that was about it.

When he came to a stable position, no further boxes raining from the sky, he opened his squeezed-shut eyes and saw nothing but darkness. He felt with his whiskers and realized he was inside a small box. He pushed the walls, then when none opened, he figured out the box was upside down and he sat on the top.

Great. He'd just invented the perfect mousetrap. How the hell was he getting out of this? The easiest way was to shift. He hoped the janitor lady wasn't on her way down. All he needed was some random female checking out his junk.

His animal relented control and Russel shifted. The box ended up covering his head, stuck around his ears. He was about to toss it aside, but thought better of it. He picked up the busted camera collar and headed for an exit. His mission was accomplished. The cat lady was here.

Sirens sounded in the distance. Seemed Devin had enough video evidence to call Chief Charter to get a crew over here to clean up the kitty litter. Russel snuggled the box around his cock and balls and opened a back door, setting off the alarm.

CHAPTER THIRTY-FIVE

Devin stood in front of the utility building with Chief Charter and Director Milkan. The sun had just set, and the plethora of emergency vehicles' lights made it feel like a disco.

"What I haven't figured out," Charter said, "is how the money got out of the bank without anyone seeing it."

Devin grinned. "That's another genius idea. Charli mentioned how the bags they found in the buried container smelled like spoiled food and had sauce smears on them. After the cat woman bagged the money, she dropped the tied sacks in the lunchroom trash cans. Nobody is going to dig through one of those unless they have to. Then the next morning, after leaving in cat form—"

Charter finished. "She came back as the cleaning lady and took out the trash."

"Exactly," Devin said.

Director Milkan slapped him on the back. "Damn proud of you, Sonder. Mighty fine detective work. I knew you'd be perfect for the position with us. Glad you decided to sign on."

"Thank you, Milkan. So am I." For the first time in a long time, he felt satisfaction from taking down a bad guy. Or woman.

The front door to the business opened and a slew of police surrounded the female wrapped in a blanket. Her long stringy hair fell over her face, hiding any identifying features.

Director Milkan stepped away. "Excuse me for a moment. I want to make sure our thief is treated properly and not mishandled in any way." He walked toward the group heading to the back of a squad car.

Charter stared at the group. "I still have a lot of unanswered questions for the lady. Like how she got the glass cutter to cut the hole in the jeweler's case into the building if she was let in as a cat. Why is she a missing person from the East Coast? Did she fake her death to become a thief? And why, in the name of God, did she do all this just to set up a customer in their system?"

"That's a very good question only she can answer, I'm afraid. The record on the computer was deleted when we got in to investigate earlier," Devin replied. A car door slammed, and Devin looked up to see Milkan headed to them, the rest of the men already gone. "How is she?"

Milkan grunted. "Not talking. Like usual with these kinds of people." Milkan looked at him. "I assume you will get the answers from her in the morning? There's a lot of mystery around her and her past. Plus, I want to know if she was involved in the armored truck robbery and murder. We have little to go on there."

They watched as a female officer opened the door to the back of the car holding their thief. She laid a set of scrubs on the woman's lap and closed the door. "Good," Milkan added. "We got her clothes to put on before she gets to the station."

Chief Charter looked around sheepishly, then leaned closer to Milkan. "Was your boy really a rat?"

Milkan looked around for Mayer. He wasn't hard to find—he was following Detective Gibbons like a puppy on a string. "Well, Chief. Right now, I'd call him a hound dog. But your detective may call him a pest. Really, though, he's probably able to be all of the above. A multishifter can do and be anything."

Director Milkan sighed. "Seems like you have it well in control here, Sonder. I'll be on my way to get started with the weekend. Get this circus wrapped up and out of here. Show's over. Make sure the crime scene is secure until forensics leaves. Have a fabulous weekend. Don't call me unless you're dead."

Devin replied, "You got it, Boss."

Charter stepped toward the police car securing the suspect. "Let's talk to our lady, then get her booked at the station. Milkan is right. Time to get this show on the road." He opened the door the female police officer had closed a few minutes ago. The woman inside sat with her head leaned back, staring at the roof's interior. Her mouth gaped.

Devin didn't like how this looked. He approached the car she'd been put in. He placed a hand on the blanket on her shoulder. Her body slid to the side and slumped over. Devin reached in to grab her while Charter yelled to the remaining EMTs packing up the ambulance.

Devin checked for a pulse at the base of her jaw. The beat was strong. He held her head in his hands and tapped on her cheek. She was still unresponsive, eyes never focusing, her body limp with no muscle control.

Medics arrived with a gurney. Devin ran through physical symptoms as he swapped places with the lead EMT. The medical technician flashed a light in her eyes. "Not good." He pulled out of the car. "Let's get her to the hospital. No pupil response."

No pupil reaction? Devin watched as they moved her from the backseat to the roller bed. "What does no pupil response mean?"

The technician frowned at him. "Serious brain damage. Coma. Death."

CHAPTER
THIRTY-SIX

Devin leaned against the water utility building, arms crossed, no smile on his face. Most of the emergency responders had left, and things were quieting down. Chief Charter followed behind the ambulance with their perp—their comatose, brain-dead perp. How the hell did that happen? Shit. They were all standing right there, a few yards from the car.

The puzzle pieces didn't fit. Hell, they weren't even from the same puzzle box. They had solved the immediate crime, but Devin knew in his gut there was more to this. A lot more.

He ran a hand through his hair, making it stick up in clumps. He was so tired right now, he didn't even care that hairs were out of place. Russel laid a hand on his shoulder. "Ready to go home? I'm bushed."

Devin smiled. "Get anywhere with your mate?"

"If you mean alone, no. If you mean friend-wise, no. If you mean anything-wise, no." A grin spread across his face. "She's playing hard to get. And I love a great hunt. And she's worth every slap in the face."

Heartache rose in Devin. He was once again reminded of what he didn't, and probably wouldn't, have.

Russel glanced at him after a sniff. "Sorry, dude. Forgot you haven't met yours yet."

"She doesn't exist," Devin said.

Russel huffed. "You can't think that way, man. You have to be positive. I mean, look. Fate brought me here to meet my mate. You are on your path. You're working your way toward her."

Time to change the subject as far as he was concerned. "Tell me about the woman. Did you get anything from her?"

Russel thought for a moment. "She was zombified at the computer. Like she was on autopilot, doing something programmed into her brain. Then, when I scratched her, she snapped out of it. I think she responded wildly because I was a rat. Instincts. Somebody else and she might've been fine."

"Why was she at the computer in the first place?" Devin said out loud to himself.

"Maybe she wanted free water and was setting up her account. I mean, who better to hide an account than a person who knows all the secrets to finding them?" Russel asked.

"Shit, Mayer. You may have something there. Not only a free account, but someone who is using enough water to warrant being checked on. Someone who doesn't want anyone to know what they're up to. There's another person involved."

Devin thought back to the info from the DC group. The woman had been a missing person from across the country. If he remembered correctly, they told him and Russel that she was human. Well, they got that part wrong. She was definitely a shifter. And where was the money and jewels?

"Mayer, what do you know about the armored truck incident?"

"Not much. Haven't even seen the scene yet. When Milkan called earlier, he mentioned the truck was forced off the road. Then human and bear footprints were found leading to the creek not too far away. We'll know more when we get evidence results next week."

"Want to drive around with me for a little while?"

Russel looked at his watch. "Yeah. It's only 7:30 p.m. At *night*. On a Friday. Before Saturday, a day off. Let's cruise Main."

Devin grimaced. "Right, sorry. I forgot I'm not in LA anymore."

"No, dude. You gotta rest or you'll wear yourself down. You will burn out." Russel paused, then said, "And that's why you're here in Oregon, isn't it? You were burned so badly, you considered everything a waste of time. Even breathing."

Devin stared at Russel for a second. He saw a spark of kinship in his coworker's words. Russel may have been a horny shifter who seemed anything but professional, but he went much deeper than that. Devin had a feeling that others saw only what Russel wanted them to see. Maybe fate did play a part.

"Yeah, well. It's late," Devin said. "Better to go home. You're right. See you Monday."

Russel watched him walk away. "Shit. Wait! My car's at the department."

CHAPTER
THIRTY-SEVEN

Saturday morning, Charli stood in the hospital's patient pick-up area while Barry opened the front passenger door to Detective Gibbons's car.

"Detective Gibbons—" Charli started.

"Please, call me Tamara. Detective Gibbons is reserved for Agent Mayer only." Both ladies laughed. The back door closed, and Barry scooted to the middle of the backseat.

"Okay, Tamara. Thank you so much for coming to get us. With the shooter still out there, I— We don't feel safe anywhere." Charli glanced at Barry in the back.

Tamara gave her a quizzical look. "I guess nobody told you. We found a rifle in the vehicle that ran you off the road. We don't have any ballistics to compare marks, but we're thinking he's your guy."

Charli laid her head back against the seat. Relief poured through her, almost making her tear up. She'd never been in a situation where someone was trying to kill her. Repeatedly. She didn't realize the stress she was carrying until the second it was gone.

"I know there is at least one bullet in my house's siding on the back porch. We can bring it Monday for your lab."

"That would be great. We share forensic equipment and people with other counties since we're small and usually pretty quiet. The team works weekends at our lab when needed and two others during the week. So it will be several days before we get results back."

Barry spoke up from the back. "But you feel certain this is the man. He came after us twice. I will keep Charli in hiding all week if I have to."

Tamara smirked and looked sideways at her. "Lucky woman." Both ladies giggled. Barry's face turned red. Charli thought he looked so adorable. She *was* a very lucky woman. Russel told her what having a shifter mate meant. He would love and protect her to his dying day. His eyes, heart, and mind would never roam to another female. He would always find her desirable no matter what she looked like—old and wrinkly, scrawny and pale.

Was that true? It sounded too good. Way too good. She found it hard to believe. Time would tell.

"So, where are we going first? New car dealership or the tow truck lot?" Tamara asked.

Charli turned to Barry. "I thought we could get our stuff for the hotel out of the back of the truck, then we can take a cab to the dealership downtown later."

"Great idea, babe. You're going to be sore for a while, so later would be good. After a long soak in the hotel's hot tub." That did sound like heaven, as long as a naked bear sat with her. Barry sucked in a deep breath and his fingers dug into his legs. A low grumble filled the air.

"Have they learned anything else about the guy who shot us? Like who he was or why he was after us?"

"Unfortunately, no," Tamara said. "The body was too mangled to get much."

"What?" Barry and Charli said together.

"It seems that in between the time you left in the ambulance and the time police arrived on the scene, a wild bear attacked the body and did some hefty damage to the head and limbs."

Charli gave him a questioning look and he shrugged, not having a clue what Tamara was talking about. They continued silently until pulling into the tow truck facility. Her SUV was so smashed, she barely recognized it. She wondered how she survived such a horrible crash. Emotions flooded her chest. She felt as though she could barely catch her breath.

Barry reached forward and put a comforting hand on her shoulder. "You're safe, my love. I'll be here to make sure nothing else happens. I'd give my life for yours." She wiped away the wetness on her cheek and nodded.

Tamara pulled up to the chain-link fence and parked the car. They climbed out as the front door to the small aluminum building opened. "Howdy, Detective Gibbons. Good to see you again," the man coming down the sidewalk said.

"Hello, Mr. Donnelly. Good to see you, too. I have the owner of the black SUV you pulled in last night. She'd like to get what she can from the vehicle."

"Should be fine," he said. He put a key into the padlock around the gate and popped it open. "Both vehicles were released from evidence before I brought them in."

Barry took her hand and led her forward. Her other hand covered her mouth as if that would hold back the mountain of emotion rolling through her. The roof of the SUV almost pressed the top of the seats, it had been smashed so low. The passenger front door was jammed opened. Only the strength of a shifter would've been able to force the bent metal.

The driver's side window was busted away. She didn't remember how she got out of the truck. Only that she called Milkan and shot at a bear attacking her mate. A bear dragged off by another in a very short time span.

Barry busted out what was remaining of the back window and brushed away the scattered glass pieces. He reached in and pulled out two suitcases. Charli climbed onto the passenger seat and searched the inside for her purse and phone. She also snagged the registration papers and insurance from the glove box. She'd need all that later. She didn't want to deal with it now.

"Hey, Tamara," Barry called from behind the SUV, "would a bullet still embedded in the door work for forensics testing to match gun marks?"

The women joined Barry to see what they had. The lift gate had a deep dent in which the bullet looked wedged.

"Looks like it's not damaged that much. We could probably use it."

Barry squeezed and jammed his fingers into the indent and pried out the slug. "You said forensics were at your lab today. Do you think they could do a quick test to see if there is a heavy possibility one way or the other that this bullet and their gun match?"

Tamara shrugged. "All we can do is ask."

CHAPTER
THIRTY-EIGHT

Charli and Barry followed Tamara through the halls of the Shedford Police Department. For a Saturday, there was more activity than Charli anticipated. But criminals don't take weekends off, so neither can the police.

They reached an area with smaller stations that looked like they housed equipment for specific purposes. A lot of microscopes and extra-bright lights, beakers, tubes, computer monitors. Some looked similar to stuff at FAWS, but here there was just a lot more of . . . everything.

Tamara knocked on a glass door, then proceeded inside to find a man wearing goggles, blue gloves, and a white lab coat. She stopped abruptly and crossed her arms over her chest. Out loud she said, "Is that the most unprofessional, lamest excuse for an examiner you've ever seen? I mean, look at him."

Charli and Barry shared a concerned look, both speechless. Charli assumed their chances of getting a quick test was about zilch now. She was ready to sneak out before the guy noticed them.

Milly Taiden

The examiner had salt-and-pepper hair, closely trimmed. When he spun around and whipped off his clear safety glasses, she noted deeply etched crow's feet around his eyes. Probably from squinting into microscopes all his life.

Charli braced for a verbal knock-down, drag-out fight. Maybe this wasn't a good idea. Then Barry smiled. She about elbowed him in the ribs when Tamara wrapped her arms around the man. He hugged her in return.

"Hello, baby girl. I was wondering if I was going to see you today. Your mother is expecting you for dinner, you know."

Tamara stepped back from the technician. "I know, Dad. I'm helping out a friend today. Sort of official, but not totally." She gestured to them. "Dad, this is Charli Avers with FPU Oregon, and this is Barry . . ." Her expression said she didn't know Barry's last name. Which was fine, since he currently didn't have one. Charli hadn't shared much about Barry with her yet. "Uh, just Barry, I guess."

They each shook hands with Tamara's dad. "Frank Gibbons. Nice to meet you both." Frank looked to his daughter again. "Since you are sorta official, I'm assuming you'd like something off the record, but not totally." He smiled at his daughter rolling her eyes.

"Dad, you make me sound like a fugitive trying to sneak evidence out."

He feigned surprise. "What? My daughter do something not by the book? How dare she?"

She laughed nervously. "Okay, Dad. Now you're embarrassing me."

He chuckled, unperturbed by her bright blushing. "Isn't that what parents are for?"

"Yeah, yeah. We need your expertise. Put that AFTE training to use."

Her dad smiled brightly, almost like a kid in a toy store. "Do we get to test-shoot guns in the tank?"

Tamara pulled out a tissue from her coat pocket to reveal the bullet taken from the back of the truck. "Only if you get Mom to make pudding for dessert tonight. Butterscotch."

He grabbed tweezers from the table and carefully lifted the item from the tissue. He held it up and eyeballed it. "I'll make pudding if it comes down to that." He turned the slug side to side. "This was shot from quite a distance. Was it stuck in the side of a vehicle? Looks a couple days old, exposed to the weather. The vehicle was driving away when the bullet hit, yes?"

Tamara looked at Charli and Barry. Astounded, Charli fumbled out, "How do you know all that?"

"My dad"—Tamara stood straighter, pride in her voice—"is a certified Firearm and Tool Mark Examiner. He received the National Lab Analyst of the Year three times, won the Goddard Award for Excellence, and has published several highly rated resources for the firearm industry."

Charli wondered if she should warn Russel about his mate's dad's expertise with guns. Nope. Let him find out the good old-fashioned way. When he got chased down by her father.

Her dad preened under the attention. "And I hit a hole in one at the Shedford public golf course two years ago."

Tamara huffed. "Dad, you treat that stupid golf thing as if it's the culmination of your life's work."

"When you get to be my age, you will understand, daughter. Until then, we have guns to shoot."

After Tamara returned from signing out the rifle from the evidence room, her dad filled out papers and attached them to a folder. "Might as well do this by the book so it's official. Don't want to do it again."

He picked up the rifle and ran a finger down its length. "Gun barrels are made with grooves along the inside that make shooting more accurate. It's like throwing a football. A spiral is much better than a wobbly throw.

"Now, inside the grooves are marks called striations. These striations make every gun barrel like a snowflake: unique. So when we have two bullets that have the same striation pattern etched into them, then it's more than likely the bullets were shot from the same gun."

Frank turned to a microscope with two glass plates at the bottom. "This is a comparative microscope. It allows us to analyze both bullets at the same time to see if they match." Tweezers in hand, he placed the slug from the SUV on one of the plates. When he flipped a couple of switches, the image from the microscope appeared on a screen on the wall.

On the bullet, he pointed to a row of vertical lines that varied in height and distance from each other. "Those different lines are the striation marks from the barrel." He lifted the gun from the table. "Now the fun part. Follow me."

They walked to the back corner of the room where a metal box the size of a big casket sat on the floor. Frank loaded the rifle, slid the barrel through an opening in the front of the box, and pulled the trigger. Barely any sound was heard.

After setting the gun on a side table, he lifted the lid to reveal water filling the inside. He fished the test bullet from the unit and placed it under the microscope on the second glass plate. A second image showed on the overhead screen.

Immediately they could see the lines on each bullet were identical in all the striations. Frank did a few more things, then turned off the scope. "There are more tests to run, obviously, but I would say this gun, more than likely, shot the bullet found in your truck."

His words set off a reaction in Charli that she didn't expect. Her knees wanted to give, relief and happiness fought for the tears in her eyes, and the tightness around her chest released. Barry wrapped her in his strong arms and rocked with her, whispering softly into her ear.

They were safe.

CHAPTER THIRTY-NINE

Charli dragged her worn-out suitcase through the hotel room door. She dropped it at the foot of the bed, then collapsed onto the bouncy mattress.

After the attack at the house and being run off the road, she didn't want to be isolated at her house. Instead, they were staying the night at a posh—for Shedford—hotel in town. Fortunately, no cows were sick that day or going into labor yet. Maybe this weekend she would be free the entire time.

She racked her brain trying to figure out who the hell the guy was shooting at them. Neither she nor Barry recognized the person. Barry seemed to be the target, but in both instances she'd been shielded. The first time with the SUV, she being on the driver's side, and the second, on the far side of the porch.

Charli fully believed the attack that shot Barry in his cute ass wasn't a local person protecting their property. Whoever he was, he aimed to kill, not scare. The police had no idea who the deceased bear shifter was, nor were there any missing persons reported locally.

Did the person know her, or did he find her from the tracking device on her truck? She'd worked with so many clients over the years, she felt secure in thinking she'd met nearly everyone around the area.

"Barry, I just thought of something."

He laid down the smaller suitcase and credit card they'd reserved the room with. "What's that, my love?"

"If the shooter took the buried container, would it be logical to think he took the money bags, too?"

"Works for me." He bent over her body, half on the bed, her feet on the floor, and began to unbutton her blouse and front-clasp bra.

"So does that clear you of everything? You have no stolen goods. The cat woman was the robber by herself. There is nothing to charge you for."

"Agreed." He unfastened her pants and pulled off undies and all with one swipe.

She grinned. He was so focused, so intent, so cute. "This reminds me that we need to buy you clothes. Not that I mind you being naked all the time. But you'll need stuff for several days."

He slid the shirt over his head. His chest rippled with each movement. "Later. I'm going to sit right here between your legs and listen while you go on." Desire slipped through her.

She shoved him back and grinned. "Not so fast, sexy bear. I'd like to check out the merchandise first."

Barry raised his brows, and she had to bite her lip to keep from giggling. She shoved him back on the bed, her hand going straight for his pants. Need coiled in her belly, warming her to the core. A single tug and the pants were down his hips, his cock springing free for her to see.

Oh yes. She'd been thinking about this, which said what kind of a nympho she was, but she didn't care. She lowered to her knees, curling her fingers over his velvety smooth hardness. He sucked in a breath and a low rumble sounded from him.

She licked her lips and came within an inch of his cock. "Tell me to suck you."

He blinked, his gorgeous lips curving into a sinful smile. "Open your gorgeous lips and take it all, you dirty girl."

She grinned, unable to stop herself, and shook her head. "Someone's been watching porn."

He shrugged. "It's the only thing I could think of. Now, go on. Suck my dick. You have the lips for it."

She should be offended, but the fact that he called her lips gorgeous thrilled her. She licked up from root to tip, flicking her tongue over the rim and taking with it the bead of liquid at the slit.

"Ah, baby. That feels fucking amazing."

She did it again, licking and sucking him into her mouth, using her tongue to massage him, and slowly drove him down her throat. She pulled back, leaving his cock slick with her spit. She twirled her tongue around his cock in circles, using her saliva and his pre-cum to lubricate his length before opening wide and sucking him into her mouth.

"God, Charli. Your mouth is heaven. Pure bliss."

Taking him into her mouth again, she felt his fingers glide into her hair, gripping her long strands away from her face. The way he groaned every time she sucked him deep and flicked her tongue over the head of his cock was making her get soaked.

"Stop!"

She did as he asked and he gently pulled her face away from his glistening shaft.

"Is everything okay?" Damn, she hoped she hadn't fucked that up.

His face said she'd done good. He leaned down and cupped her face, kissing her in a hot and desperate manner she wasn't used to but totally loved. When he left her lips, he growled softly. "Everything is fucking perfect, but I can't wait to shove my face between your legs."

Really, what woman in her right mind would argue with that?

They switched places on the bed. She sat on the edge, her legs wide open, and Barry went down on his knees staring hungrily between her thighs. There was no need for words. He dove in, lavishing her folds with sucks and licks.

She squealed and lay flat on her back. He pushed her legs up. She crossed her legs at the ankles, pressing her heels into his back. The man was a genius with tongue usage.

"Keep licking me. I'm so hot. I need you," she said, her voice low and garbled.

His tongue danced over her clit, down to her entrance, and even lower to her ass. Then he did it again. She gripped the bedding and moaned loudly, no longer caring if anyone heard them. Fuck it! Let the entire county hear them.

Lust burned through her veins. She gasped at the quick tightening of her muscles. The orgasm caught her completely by surprise. His licks and sucks on her pussy turned faster, harsher.

Tension snapped inside her. She pressed her head back, her chest rising with the bowing of her back. Her body lost control. She screamed. The burning call for him rushed up her throat and left her lips at the same time a wave of bliss blasted her.

She'd never, not even when she'd played with herself with her countless toys, come as hard as she had that moment.

Barry lifted his head from between her legs. A sexy smile flirted over his lips. "I knew you'd taste good. Like fucking honey."

She licked her lips, laughing at his choice of words. "Honey, bear?"

He nodded. "Oh yeah. I can't wait to dip my cock into your honey pot."

She snorted, watching him rise, his body looming above. "Sounds like a plan."

She rose, watching him sit on an ottoman at the foot of the bed and proceed to jerk his cock in his hand. "Come here, beautiful. I have something for you."

Laughter bubbled up her throat. "Is it a banana?"

His grin widened to show beautiful white teeth. "Sure. Let's see how you like my banana dipping into your cream."

She went around the bed, coming to stop in front of him and immediately straddling his legs. His hands gripped her waist as she slid down, impaling herself on him. She continued down in a single glide until they were pressed together, pelvis to pelvis. "Barry," she groaned, her arms going around his neck and pulling his face to hers. "I love your banana in my cream."

He kissed her, licking her lip and nibbling on her jaw. "I love every single thing about you."

She rocked her hips and took a small lick of his skin and felt her pussy squeeze.

Breaths rushed out of her lungs in a race out of her body.

"God, baby. That's just what I like." He groaned, his hands tight around her hips. "Squeeze my dick with your tight little pussy," he grunted.

She wiggled her body back and forth. She didn't get a chance to do much. He lifted and dropped her on his cock repeatedly. She bounced on him, her pussy taking his heated shaft deeply and lifting until it was almost out of her, only to drop again. The lifts and drops didn't slow. They increased with speed and strength. She couldn't keep up. He was in control. Pressing her down so she could grind her pussy on his pelvis. Every drop felt like she was being branded from the inside.

"God," she moaned. "This feels amazing!"

"You're amazing, my beautiful mate."

She bit her lip and moaned. "Barry . . ."

"I like how slick your pussy is." He let her control the rocking at that point. She wiggled faster and faster on him, weaving her body like a snake, back and forth and pressing down on his cock. "I like how you do that. Your whole body is taking my cock, not just your slick pussy." He grasped her face with one hand and met her gaze, his eyes bright with a feral look. "I like that you like me fucking you. That you want me coming deep in your pussy, making you mine all over again."

"I like that, too." She didn't understand it, but there was no denying it.

"How about I put my seed into your pussy?" He pressed her down again, rocking her over his shaft. "I want you mine. Every day of my life."

"God, yes!"

He slid a hand between her legs to fondle her clit. "Tell me, baby. Tell me you're mine."

That was hard to think about when all her body wanted was for her to come. All she could visualize was the explosion of pleasure when she finally did. But the way he took her body and owned her showed her that both the human and animal sides in him wanted her. "Yes, Barry. I'm yours. All yours."

He pressed at her clit hard, pinching her, and her body convulsed with the force of her orgasm. She curved her back, pressing her chest into his body, plastering them together. He continued lifting and dropping her, even though she had lost the ability to control her body. Then he slowed, holding her still as he came along with her, pushing her toward another orgasm faster than ever.

He growled loudly, his body vibrating under hers as he came, filling her with his seed.

"You're mine!"

"Yes! Yes!" She choked on each word as she struggled to take in air while riding the wave of her orgasm. Barry, her Barry, was a miracle worker. He'd gotten her to come more times than ever.

It was long moments before she could move. They were both breathing choppy breaths as he pulled out of her. She knew there was no giving this up. Not Barry or the emotions he brought out in her. She knew one thing for sure—no matter what came, they'd face it together. Barry was no longer just some bear that needed her help. He was her mate. He was the man for her. She'd do anything for him. She loved him, and together they would figure out what had happened to his memory. At least they knew he wasn't a criminal, not that there had been any doubt in her mind. She'd known deep inside he was innocent.

CHAPTER FORTY

C harli woke, but didn't open her eyes yet. She didn't want to let go of the happiness and peacefulness she felt when in Barry's arms. These emotions were almost foreign to her. She was content with her life, loved working with the animals, but there was nothing that took her to the next level. To the place where she felt energized and wanted to do the fun, crazy things love made you do.

Whoa. The L word. She'd never used it before. A few guys in college interested her, but they got boring with their constant frat mentality. She wanted more than drunken bashes and puke on her shoes.

Was she ready for the L word? She laughed at herself. She couldn't even say the damn word. Was that a clue? But memories of the past sixty hours—shit, only two and a half days?—played in her mind. The way he looked at her with such desire and longing. The way his lips hitched up on the side when he was teasing. The way his bear called her "mate." So sure and natural. She felt the truth. Or did she imagine it, overwhelmed by all that happened that Thursday morning before even one cup of coffee?

Then there was the stolen money, even if he didn't take it. How did he fit in? He was in a zombie state when he packed the money bags from the boat. Was he under some kind of mind control? She knew he didn't take the loot from their hiding spots. He'd been with her constantly or locked in the cage after the armored truck heist. So the other player *had* to be the shooter, and he must've taken the money. Was she trying to convince herself?

Charli noticed the hotel room was too quiet. This closed in, she'd hear Barry's breathing at least. Her eyes sprang open and she sat up. "Barry." No reply. She threw off the covers and skittered to the bathroom. Empty with lights off. "Barry?" Just to make sure he wasn't playing a joke on her, she looked in the closet and under the bed.

Charli sat on the sheets, tears welling. He had left a second time. Would she ever see him again? The pain in her chest took her breath away. The thought of not having him in her life made her ache. She was convinced; she loved him on a level that went beyond the mental bond of marriage. Her soul was attached to the man. But he'd left her.

She fell back on the bed, letting her arms plop next to her head. Her hand hit something that rumpled. After rolling over, she saw a note on the hotel's notepad resting on the other pillow. *Meet me in the hotel restaurant.*

Charli heaved a breath and collapsed onto the mattress. He didn't leave her. He was still in the building. How long had she been asleep? Outside was twilight.

She jumped off the bed, showered, dressed as best she could with the clothes thrown into the suitcase, then headed to the restaurant on the fifth floor.

Barry overlooked the town from his fifth-floor private balcony in the restaurant. He liked this small-town atmosphere. Everyone seemed friendly. He didn't have problems getting around.

He wondered where he was from. What his life had been like. Did he have a job? Was he married with kids? The thought sent shock waves through him. The idea of a family had come up earlier, but holy fuck. He prayed he didn't have a family somewhere waiting for him to return home. Who would he give up? The wife and children who had loved him for years and probably depended on him? Or Charli, the self-sustained, confident, independent woman? He wasn't liking the obvious answer.

Then he wondered what he had to do with the money and killing the guard in the armored truck. Was he a trained killer, assigned to take out targets on order? Was he a thief, stealing money from the armored truck? Would he spend the rest of his life in jail, away from the woman he loved?

Wait. He loved her? *Mate.* They'd known each other for only a few days. But, yes, he did love her. It felt right. It felt natural. He wanted a family with her. His insides were craving babies, lots of them. Wow. He wondered if he should be worried about that. Did Charli want a family? Children? It was probably too soon to ask her. He didn't want her to freak out.

And if all that wasn't enough, he didn't know any of this shifter stuff Charli kept referring to. He felt the creature inside, but it didn't seem to be a part of him. Like a spirit had taken up residence in his head, rarely showing itself. Devin and Russel had spoken to him briefly about being a shifter, but it didn't make a lot of sense at the time.

The fancy fountains in front of city hall danced with lights, making a fun display to watch. Twilight had descended over the town. He looked around for a clock. Charli should've been up by now. Maybe he should check on her.

When he turned to the restaurant's main floor, he saw the most beautiful woman he'd ever seen. Well, since the other day and his new self. Her natural beauty shone from within. She glowed with little makeup and glittered without gaudy, ostentatious jewelry. His heart stuttered. Yes, this was the only woman for him.

The hostess opened the glass French doors to the balcony and gestured Charli through. She was radiant. He brought her hand to his lips. She smelled divine. *Mate.* That was at least the third time he'd heard that word from the visitor in his head. If said visitor mumbled it one more time without adding some sort of explanation with it, he'd kick its ass.

The image of a bear flipping its tail at him as it walked away flashed in his mind. He'd think about all that later. Right now, he had a pretty woman with him on a perfect night, with chilled wine and stuffed mushrooms waiting on the table.

"I trust you slept well, beautiful." He pulled her into his arms and they swayed to the soft music in the background.

Her smile was dazzling. "I did, thank you for asking. And I must say you look incredible." She stepped back to take him in. "How did you know guys in boots and jeans with a sport coat is my favorite look?" Her eyes stopped on his chest.

It embarrassed him a bit. But since his eyes lingered on her chest all the time, turnabout was fair play. "Not to mention a T-shirt that shows every nook and cranny." She licked her lips, sending an electric jolt through him. Shit, he was getting hard again. He wondered how well those inside could see them.

"I had to entertain myself so you could sleep, so I went shopping. The town is homey. Nice place to live. Oh, one day I'll pay you back for what I put on your credit card."

Charli leaned back and laughed. "So that's how you did it. Seems the town isn't very security cautious if they didn't ask for ID."

"Actually, they were, a little. The cashier rang up the total and looked at the name on the card. I told her the card company left off the *e* on my first name. I told her a new one was in the mail."

She playfully slapped him on the arm. "You are such a schemer."

He pulled her closer and whispered in her ear, "Guess what I have scheming in my mind, right now, sexy lady." He turned so her backside faced out, then slid his hand to cup her round ass and pressed her against his hard cock. "Fuck, woman. You are so damn enthralling. I want to be buried balls deep in you now. I can barely hold back. My other half is pressing, too, wanting to fuck you senseless."

Barry kissed her along the throat with a sudden urge to bite her at the base of her neck and shoulder. Where the fuck did that come from? He wouldn't bite her on purpose.

His hand glided up her back into her hair as they continued to shift side to side with the music. His thoughts went back to a few minutes ago before Charli arrived. He realized the old him was dead. Gone with all the memories that went with it. He needed to focus on the future instead of the past.

"Charli, can I tell you something without you freaking out and shoving me over the balcony?"

She leaned back, eyes wide. "Do you remember something from your past?"

He grinned and shook his head, no longer saddened by the fact that he couldn't remember. "More than that. I see my future, love. It's you. I want you. For now. For the future. For always. Without you, life isn't worth living for me. My past is irrelevant. The person I was is gone. You've gotten to know me. The real me. You know my heart, Charli. It's yours. Beats only for you.

"Please promise me that whoever I was or whatever I did won't scare you away. Please, Charli. I don't ever want to be without you." He steeled himself for the worst. "I guess I'm asking you to marry me. Eventually. Once I have an identity again."

Her body stiffened against him. Fuck, that wasn't good. He kept quiet, letting her absorb everything his heart poured out.

Charli didn't say she wouldn't freak out, but she wasn't anyway. Her heart felt lightened like a weight of pending doom had been avoided.

He was right. The person he was no longer existed. She communicated with his bear and felt the good in him, the genuine love in him.

She also remembered how she almost died, thinking Barry had left her in the hotel room. That told her the truth of her heart. What the brain said was important, but she could control her brain. Her heart, she could not.

She looked into his shiny eyes. "Barry, I agree with all you said. It takes a real man to put himself out there like that and not be worried about rejection."

"Never said I wasn't worried over here. I'm about to shit my pants." Barry cupped her face with his big hands. "Promise me, sweetheart, you won't leave. I love you."

Aw damn, she was about to cry, he was so sweet. So many emotions swirled around her, all making her want to jump up and down screaming *yes*. And she loved him. No questioning what her heart said.

It was insane to think true love could happen in three days, but when you had the right person, the one person who touched the deepest parts of your soul, how could you *not* know immediately? He was the person her heart and soul recognized as *the one*, at first sight. And for those who didn't want to believe, fine. Because she was happy and in love.

"You know, when I saw you and the other bear fighting and you were about to become bug food, I nearly lost it. I couldn't imagine my life without you. I didn't realize how alone I'd been until you showed up. And now," she took a deep breath, letting the shaking in her hands calm down. "I won't let you go."

She wasn't afraid to say it any longer. "Barry Bear, I love you and will marry you. Eventually."

EPILOGUE

Charli glanced at Barry with a smile. Maybe he'd remember his life soon. She'd love to know more about him, the original him. He was such a great guy, but she knew deep down that no matter what he said, he would always feel like something was missing until he finally knew his past.

Barry glanced up from the salad he'd helped chop and grinned. Man, she really loved him. There wasn't a doubt in her mind he'd do anything to protect her.

He dropped the knife and wiped his hands on a kitchen towel. She placed the lid back on her stew and turned to face him.

"What are you thinking about, my beautiful mate?" He wrapped his hands around her waist, their bodies flush together.

"I was hoping you'd start to remember your past. For your own peace of mind."

He nodded and met her gaze, the gold from his bear always right under the surface. "It doesn't matter. I'd like to remember, but if I don't, it won't change how I feel about you, sweetheart. I love you."

She lifted her face and brushed her lips over his. "I know. I love you, too."

Her only hope now was that once his memory returned, there weren't going to be other obstacles in their way. Her gut told her there was a lot more coming.

ACKNOWLEDGMENTS

This book wouldn't be possible without some amazing people supporting me.

My Readers – Thank you

Tina Winograd – Your intelligence helps me tremendously when I'm writing. Thank you for dropping everything and getting back to me right away. You don't know how much you are appreciated for all you do.

Mr. T (aka Hubby) – Thank you for pushing me and believing I can rule the world. One day, I just might.

My Kids – Aiden, for your love and random (only when you want) hugs. Alan, for sitting with me while I write, to keep me focused (it mostly worked). Angie, for the cute emoji messages (I love the little whale). You can be anything. I know; I'm proof of that.

Bianca – Where have you been all my life? We all need that one friend that makes life brighter. You're it.

Julie – For your unwavering support and willingness to read anything I send you. No matter how bad it looks.

My Girls: Jennifer – For your help. Sheri – For your love and time. Teracia – For the midnight encouragement. Nicole – For all the cake. Jessica – For your continued support. Bambi – For making my life easier. Heather – For keeping me on track.

My Street Team and Curvy Reader Group – Thank you all for your support and telling everyone about my books. It's massively appreciated!

ABOUT THE AUTHOR

 Milly Taiden is the *New York Times* and *USA Today* bestselling author of numerous series, including the Sassy Mates books and the Federal Paranormal Unit novels. Milly loves writing sexy stories so hot they sizzle your e-reader. When her curvy humans meet their furry alphas, inhibitions give way to animal instincts—and carnal desire. She lives in Florida with her husband, child, and Needy Speedy, their spunky dog. Milly is addicted to shoes, Dunkin' Donuts, and chocolate and is aware she's bossy. Visit her online at www.millytaiden.com.